THE SACRIFICE OF MENDLESON MOONY

MARK FASSETT

OTHER BOOKS BY
MARK FASSETT

A Wizard's Work
Shattered
* Fragments
* Reworked

Lords of Genova
Questioner's Shadow

* Forthcoming

THE SACRIFICE OF MENDLESON MOONY

MARK FASSETT

RAVENSTAR PRESS
MONROE, WA

Published 2012 by Ravenstar Press
Monroe, WA
http://www.ravenstarpress.com

Trade paper edition designed by Mark Fassett
in Scribus

Electronic editions designed by Mark Fassett
using StoryBox software
http://www.markfassett.com
http://www.storyboxsoftware.com

Cover art by Joe Slucher
http://www.joeslucher.com

ISBN: 978-0615606224

For Kris and Dean.
Without you, this book would not exist.
I hope the end makes more sense now.

ONE

In the mind of Mendleson Moony, the mid-summer festival was an utter waste of time. He ought to be home, working his small farm, or down on the waterfront trading his services with the fishermen who had a need for someone who could help mend boats or nets. Anything other than frolicking and celebrating for an entire day.

Around him, the town-folk cavorted and competed, heedless of his distaste for the entire affair. Contests abounded. Archery, races, tests of strength. Merchants had their wagons and carts set up to sell their wares. A dozen boars roasted over an enormous fire pit. Children raced in and out among the adults' legs with orders to slow down going unheeded.

A large, flat area remained clear. Musicians were setting up near it. The dancing would start as soon as the roasted pork had all been eaten. Mendleson looked forward to the dancing the least.

"Mendleson," a man's voice called out to him. "I didn't think you'd come."

Mendleson turned around and found his friend Paulus approaching him from the thick of the crowd. Paulus wasn't very tall, but his thick body contained more power in its muscles than most other men. He liked to show off his muscles, preferring to go without shirts whenever he could get away with it. He wore a shirt to the festival, though, surprising Mendleson.

"I almost didn't," Mendleson said. "Only the promise of a free meal brought me out."

"That and the girls, right?"

Mendleson shook his head. "You know..."

"I know. I'm sorry." Paulus reached up and put a hand on Mendleson's shoulder. He looked Mendleson straight in the eye. "But you're my friend, and I worry about you wasting away out there on your farm. You need company, my friend. You grow more and more into a ghost."

"It's only been..."

Paulus interrupted him. "It's been four years, Mendleson. You need to move on. You need to find another wife."

Four years? Has it really been that long? It seems like yesterday.

"There are plenty of women here that would be happy to have you, too," Paulus continued, while sweeping his arm out to cover the festival goers.

Mendleson looked around, and for a moment, he entertained the idea, but could not see one woman who he thought would be interested. "Point some out. I don't see any," he said.

Paulus laughed. "Fine. I'll point them out, but first, let's go find the ale. I can't be doing this without something to wet my throat."

Paulus led him off across the field toward the carts bearing large kegs. While they walked, Mendleson worked back through the years and discovered that indeed, it had been four years since he'd come home from fishing one day to find his home burned to the ground, his wife and young son burned with it.

He could remember every detail like it happened yesterday. He'd seen the smoke on the horizon as the boat landed, and he didn't think much of it until he started making his way home. About halfway there, he realized it was near his land and began to worry. When he arrived, he found his neighbors working hard to quench the flames, but there weren't enough of them.

He looked around and didn't see his wife, Mirrielle. Upon realizing she wasn't there, he tried to run in to find her, but his neighbors held him back. The house collapsed into rubble only minutes later while he cried out for her, again and again.

After the rubble cooled, they found Mirrielle and his son Josua, huddled together. He'd resolved right then to never put to sea again.

He rebuilt his home and started to farm his land in earnest. He gave up fishing.

And Paulus is right. That was *four years ago.*

They reached the ale carts. Paulus paid for mugs for the both of them, then lead Mendleson to a bench where the two of them sat and sipped their ale.

"There," Paulus said, pointing at a woman in a burgundy colored dress. She kept her dark brown hair up, and her hands close to her body. She was talking with two other women. One of the women said something, and the three of them tittered.

"Melissa Stander?" Mendleson asked.

"Right," Paulus said. "She's a widow, and I hear he did not leave her a pauper."

"Not her. She was friends with…" Mendleson didn't want to say Mirrielle's name aloud. Just seeing Melissa brought back memories. "I didn't like Melissa then. She's far too vapid."

"Fine, not her, then. How about Jessica Breach?"

Mendleson took a sip of his ale before answering. "Who's that?"

"Over there by the pork roasters." Paulus said. "I hear she's nice. Her father was a merchant, but not a good one. He tried to marry her off to a Lord from Isundry, but couldn't afford the dowry."

"The short one?"

"In the green dress and blonde hair."

Mendleson thought she was pretty. Petite, thin

boned, and delicate. For a moment, he entertained the thought, but couldn't imagine her helping with the farm.

"You must be kidding," Mendleson said. "Her father raised her with the idea of gaining a position at court. She wouldn't last a day on the farm."

Paulus nodded. "True. How about her?"

Mendleson looked where Paulus pointed and found himself looking at Fredetta Jointer. Mendleson punched Paulus in the shoulder, causing Paulus to nearly spill his ale.

"What's that for?" Paulus asked. He couldn't keep the hint of laughter out of his voice.

Mendleson laughed for the first time. It felt good. "Everyone knows she's a shrew. Her father couldn't give her away to slavers. I wouldn't even want to live in my own house!"

"It would get you back out fishing with me where you belong."

"That it would," Mendleson said, his mirth fading.

"Sorry."

"It's not your fault."

"I still should have thought... Look, forget about her. There's got to be someone here who can satisfy you."

Mendleson stood up and drank the last of his ale. "Thanks for your help, Paulus. I know you're right. I do need to find someone. I just can't forget what happened. I can't forgive myself for failing her."

Paulus stood, and pulled Mendleson around so they

were face to face. "Mendleson, my friend, you have to forgive yourself. It wasn't your fault. There was nothing you could do. It was an accident of fate."

"Fate? How could it have been fate? What good has come out of it?"

Paulus didn't answer, and Mendleson knew why. Nothing good had come out of it.

"Thanks for trying to help," Mendleson said. "I know you're right. I do need to put it behind me, but maybe I'm not ready yet."

Paulus nodded. "Look, they're taking the boars off the spits. Let's go eat. I promise I won't point out any more shrews."

Mendleson chuckled, and motioned for his friend to lead them forth. Maybe he'd feel better with food in his belly.

‡

Henrietta Swooth muttered to herself as she walked the road to the mid-summer festival. She had no real desire to go. In her three years living in the little cottage that looked out over the cliffs and onto the town below, she had not attended the festival.

But she had seen herself there. Something important would happen, and so she went. She'd learned long ago that events would conspire to put her in the places she saw herself if she tried to avoid what her visions showed her. What made it all hard to deal with is that she rarely knew why she had to go. The meaning behind her visions of herself remained a mystery.

This wasn't the case when trying to see things for the women that came to visit. She could almost always determine their fate and the reasons behind it. Sometimes, she could even see how they could do things differently to avoid the fate given to them.

But for herself, her options remained opaque.

So she found herself walking the mile and a half between her home and the festival grounds, dreading what was to come. She tried to prepare herself, as she walked, for the overwhelming number of visions that would assault her as she touched people, as she brushed them, or they her.

She looked to her right, where she could see the Western Sea, and the orange-red sun that hung low on the horizon. She'd waited until just about the right moment to leave. Her vision had her at the gathering at twilight. She didn't want to spend any more time there than necessary.

She heard the music, first. Horns, drums, and a great deal of singing, much of it out of key. It made her long for her home near the mountains.

"Put that out of your head, Henrietta," she said to herself. "You left home for good reason."

She topped a rise in the road and saw the festival ground laid out below her. Oil lamps were already lit and waiting for the sun to set. It appeared to her that most of the town had turned out.

She took a deep breath. "It's only for a short time, Henrietta," she said. Then she worked her way down the hill to join the festival.

When she first entered the grounds, she thought she might go unnoticed. Most everyone concentrated on the singing and dancing. She wandered the perimeter, looking for the place where she'd seen herself. She had time, so didn't hurry.

Which was a mistake. Three young women noticed her before she even walked twenty paces. Of course, it was always the women. The men never acknowledged that they noticed her. In her experience, men had a healthy fear of her visions. Henrietta had always thought that their reluctance was because men needed the fiction that they were in control. Surrendering to fate seemed difficult to impossible.

The women here accepted her, though. They sought her out, once it was discovered what she could do. They seemed more willing to want to work with fate, instead of against it.

Well, most of them. The women approaching her, though, had other ideas.

"Henrietta, I must ask you something."

Of course, it would be that vapid girl Melissa who wanted to know her future. *I wonder what she'll ask me this time.*

"Melissa, it is good to see you," Henrietta lied. The men suffered her here because the women liked her. She couldn't afford to upset any of them, lest the men drive her out. "What must you ask?"

"You said you saw a man coming for me, that he would be here by the end of the summer."

"It is not summer's end, yet," Henrietta said.

"I know, I know. I just wondered, with the festival and all, there are quite a few merchants from out of town. Would any of them be the one you saw?"

Well, that is a change, at least. She's given thought to accepting less than a Lord for a husband.

Henrietta looked for the merchant carts and found them, but she couldn't see through the crowd to find who manned them.

She sighed, then held out her hands. "Take hold of my hands."

Melissa smiled and reached for Henrietta's hands.

Henrietta closed her eyes, which wasn't strictly necessary. She just didn't want to watch Melissa while lying to her. She made a show of seeing the future, but as always, the girl's future was as empty as her mind.

It scared Henrietta, too. More and more often, she could see nothing in the future for the women that came to see her. She broke her contact with Melissa, not wanting to think about what it meant.

"I still see the man you hope for coming by the end of summer," she lied, "but he is not here."

Melissa's shoulders slumped in disappointment.

Henrietta understood how Melissa felt. She secretly wished for her own man to come calling, to help her give a child to the world, like her grandmother had done. But it would never be.

She looked around the festival, hoping to find some way to escape these three girls. Her gaze passed over a man she knew only from a distance. A neighbor that lived within sight of her home. She had never talked with him before, but she'd seen him working his fields, his muscles running with sweat and a permanent air of seriousness set upon his face.

Of course, she'd heard the story of what had happened to him. The women that came to her told her everything. She had locked eyes with him once, across the road, and she'd thought for a moment he might have an interest in her, but he looked away just as quick. The pain in his eyes had been near palpable.

And he was sitting right near where her vision had told her she had to be.

"Excuse me," she said, making a hasty decision. "I must go talk with someone."

Melissa ignored her, but Melissa's friends seemed to be a little put off. Henrietta didn't care. Now that she'd made her decision, she would walk over to Mendleson Moony and see what happened. *Likely nothing at all.*

✝

"Hey, look," Paulus said. "Here comes your neighbor."

Mendleson looked to where Paulus pointed. Indeed, it was his neighbor, the Seer, Henrietta Swooth. As always, she looked resplendent. Her blonde hair was bound back, but allowed to cascade onto her shoulders. The gown she wore, black with a purple trim along its arms, fit her slight frame perfectly.

When she'd arrived in town only a year after his wife died, all the single men he'd known had talked about her, wondered how she'd bought the cottage that looked over the town and the sea.

Of course, the wondering stopped as soon as wives and girlfriends started to talk of their meetings with the Seer.

Mendleson often wondered how that day would have changed if the Seer had lived across the street when his home, his life, burned. He'd thought about visiting her more than once, but in the time they'd lived across the road from each other, he'd never managed to speak a word to her.

Then Paulus hit him. "What about her? I bet she'd make a good wife for you. You'd always know what's about to happen."

"I don't think it works that way, Paulus."

"How do you know? Have you ever asked?"

Mendleson shook his head, and looked up. The Seer was almost upon them.

"Well, ask her. I need another ale." he said, then laughed and left Mendleson to stand there.

Mendleson turned to follow him. He did not want to be alone with her.

"Mendleson," she said to his back.

Just the one word, his name, stopped him. He couldn't move any further. He'd never heard her speak before. Her voice was arresting, almost magical.

He turned to face her, but couldn't open his mouth to speak. This close, she was as beautiful as he'd thought, and younger. She couldn't have been more than twenty-four or twenty-five. Of an age with his wife, had she lived.

He shook his head. *I don't want to think of that.* He made to turn and leave.

"Don't leave," she said.

"Why?"

"We've lived as neighbors for three years," she said. "I think it's time we at least said hello."

Mendleson couldn't argue with that. "You're right, of course. I've been remiss in welcoming a neighbor. I've had a difficult time of it lately."

"I know," she said.

Mendleson wasn't sure she meant to say it aloud. Her thoughts seemed to turn inward for a moment, almost as if she nursed some kind of hurt within her, too. "Here," he said "Let's at least sit on the bench."

She nodded. "Yes, let's sit."

Mendleson put his hand out to help guide her to the bench. He didn't even know why he did it. It was something he would have done for a lady he was trying to court. But he wasn't trying to court her. The gesture felt right, though.

Henrietta avoided it deftly, though, sitting on her own.

He withdrew it and sat next to her. *I wonder why she did that?*

For a while, they sat next to each other and said nothing. Mendleson let his gaze wander among the sights of the festival. The sun was just beginning to dip below the horizon. The bonfires lit the dancers in a flickering light that seemed almost unearthly.

He stole a glance at her and found her looking at him. Staring. In the low light, it was difficult to tell what color her eyes were.

"Why did you really come over here," he asked.

"I don't want to tell fortunes tonight," she said. "If I wander around by myself, the women will come up to me, one by one. Each will ask me to tell them their future, and I can't refuse."

Mendleson was puzzled. "Why can't you refuse?"

"How long do you think they would let me stay if I refused them? They suffer me because I indulge them."

"Is that why you're here? Did another town run you out?"

She laughed, but the laugh held little joy. It made

him feel warm inside, nonetheless. "No," she said. "I'm here for—other reasons."

"What other reasons?" he asked, and regretted it immediately. The smile she'd had on her lips faded.

"I'd rather not talk about them," she said. "I hope you don't mind."

"No, no. I understand." *Just like I don't want to talk about that day.*

They sat in silence for a couple minutes, listening to the music, watching the dancers. He stole glances at her, and he caught her stealing glances at him.

She intrigued him. He could tell there was pain in her past, or something akin to it. *It's probably related to her being a Seer. Not every town accepts them.*

"It must be lonely," he said.

"Sometimes. Though, at times, I find myself wishing everyone would leave me alone."

"Why?"

"The women, they come to me, all of them wanting good news. Wanting to know of long lives for their children, or wealth for themselves, or any number of silly things. They think I can give it to them, but I can only tell what I see. I don't decide their fate. It's—difficult when I have to give someone ill news."

"Does everything you see happen? Does it come true?"

She shook her head. "Things don't always come true the exact way I see them. Fates can be changed, visions misunderstood."

Fates can be changed? "Tell me," he said. "If you had been here, could you have warned me of the fire, of..."

Henrietta stood up, and Mendleson thought he'd angered her somehow. He reached out and grabbed her hand. "Please, don't go. I didn't mean..."

A flash, a spark, something, raced between them at that moment. His heart seemed to open up. At the same time, her eyes grew wide, and terror crossed her face.

She pulled away from him, stumbled backward, then fell to the ground.

Mendleson stood up and went to her. *What did I do? What did I say? What happened?*

"Here," he said, "let me help you up."

"No," she said. "Stay away from me. Stay away."

TWO

From the moment Henrietta began to talk to Mendleson, she knew she could grow to like him, perhaps more. The incident with his wife was a barrier, of course. He obviously hadn't recovered from it and blamed himself. Her heart thumped in her chest, even when he asked questions that strayed too close to subjects she'd rather not think about.

But he owned a warmth and a protectiveness that appealed to her.

If only she didn't know how her life would end. If only she hadn't learned it the day she had come into her Sight. *If only I could live with the ignorance of the unsighted.*

When he asked the question of her, asked if it would have been possible to save his wife, she'd pulled away. She knew then that he still held tight to the memory of that tragedy. She knew nothing good could come of continuing the conversation.

But he reached up and touched her hand, like she'd longed for him to do, but had refused to allow.

Her normal vision clouded, and her Sight took over at his touch. What she saw horrified her.

The monolith stands, stark and black, blotting out the night sky. The wraiths are on the plateau, coming for her. Coming to take her Sight. Coming to take her life.

A man appears and shouts something she can't hear. A man that looks strangely like Mendleson. The wraiths turn and converge on him. Circling.

They pounce. She thinks she should hear him screaming, but hears only silence. They come away from him, and turn back to her.

He is laying on the ground, not moving.

The contact with Mendleson's hand broke, ending the vision, but she had seen enough. The vision had begun like the one she saw when she gained her Sight. But now, it was different.

"Here," he said. "let me help you up."

The horror of what she'd just seen washed over her. "No," she said. "Stay away from me." She couldn't let him die, not for her. "Stay away."

She scrambled to her feet and ran. People were looking, but she didn't care.

"Henrietta," she heard him yell. "Stop, I'm sorry!"

She ignored him. She couldn't let her vision happen. It was the wrong vision. It couldn't be true. She didn't want to be responsible.

I should never have come here.

She ran all the way home in the darkness.

When she shut the door behind her, she locked it, then lit a candle. She pulled her shades, then sat down at her table to think.

"How could this happen," she asked herself. "How could he insert himself into my vision. It was *my* vision!"

She could only come up with one answer—she'd done it herself by coming to this town. "I should not have tried to avoid my fate."

She looked around the small home that had been hers for the last three years. Nicknacks, pots, and books lined her walls, overseen by a portrait of her grandmother. She put her head in her hands and tried to focus on what she should do. Tried to evoke another vision.

Her sight left her empty.

"Fine," she said. "I know what I should do, now. I know what I did wrong. I'll correct it. He doesn't deserve that fate."

She wrote a note for the grocery boy to take with him when he came. She knew what the vision meant and knew what her lack of visions for others meant. Her time was near. She couldn't see beyond her death. The end of the summer or early autumn.

She got up from the table and started sifting through her things, noting what she'd have to take and what she'd have to leave behind. She wouldn't be able to take everything.

After a moment, she grimaced. *Do I really need to take anything?*

But she couldn't make herself leave it all. Like she'd told Mendleson. Fates could be changed. *Even mine?*

‡

Mendleson lay in bed thinking about his encounter with Henrietta, and no matter how he turned it over in his head, he couldn't figure out what he'd done wrong. He'd only touched her hand, and she had pulled away violently. It was an innocent gesture, and she had reacted all out of proportion to it.

So why do I feel like I wronged her?

He couldn't come up with any answers.

And the look on her face. It was like I'd suddenly turned into a monster.

It puzzled him until he finally fell asleep.

When he woke, he remembered dreams of Henrietta Swooth. Dreams that he didn't understand. Dreams of her in trouble, running from something dark and foreboding. He remembered chasing after her, but she ran from him, too.

He climbed out of bed, ate a breakfast of bread and bacon, then went out to work his fields. He resolved, while eating, to put Henrietta out of his head. She was a strange woman. He'd thought there might be possibilities with her, but after her reaction to his touch, after she ran away, well maybe he'd been wrong.

He stepped out his front door, but couldn't help glancing across the lane toward Henrietta's home. The shades were drawn, and he didn't see any movement. *Don't be a fool, Mendleson. It's still early morning.*

He went to his barn to get his horse into its harness. As he opened the door, he realized that Henrietta had given him one thing without trying. She'd given him a night free from nightmares of Mirrielle.

The day's work proved hot and draining. The sun bore down on him, its heat a relentless opponent. He looked up occasionally from his work and didn't see a sign of her, which was unusual. He often saw her outside in her garden.

But her shades remained shut throughout the day. Even the grocery boy came and delivered sacks of groceries, but he left them on the porch to bake in the sun.

When he finished for the day, he went inside and cleaned himself up. He didn't know when it happened, but sometime during the day, he'd decided he should go and check on her and apologize for upsetting her. He couldn't get her out of his head. He hoped an apology would do the trick.

He found himself standing on her doorstep only a little while later. His stomach buzzed with butterflies and his heart thumped in his chest. *The woman did something to me. She must have.* Yesterday, all he could think of was his wife. Since he'd talked with Henrietta, all he could think of was her.

The groceries still sat on the porch, ensconced in burlap sacks. *Maybe I'll help carry them in.*

He knocked on the door and waited.

A minute passed. Two. He knocked again. More minutes passed.

"Henrietta," he called out. "Your groceries are out here in the sun."

He knocked on the door again, then put his ear to it. He heard nothing.

Mendleson gave up after a few minutes more, after it became obvious there was no one home. He told himself not to worry. *She just had a call to make in town, or something. It's not because of you.*

He descended the steps from her porch to the stone path that led through her garden to the lane. He turned back to look, and for a moment, he thought he saw one of the shades in the window move slightly. He watched for a bit. When it didn't move again, he turned back to his own house.

That night passed even slower. He couldn't get the dream from the night before out of his head. It left him with a feeling that she was in danger. He thought that's what his dream was telling him.

He tossed and turned until he decided, late in the night, that he would skip his work in the field to try to figure out what happened to Henrietta. She could be safe and hiding from him, or something could have happened. He wouldn't let the opportunity to protect her pass him by. He wouldn't let it happen again.

When the morning came, he was up soon after dawn. He ate, then went back to Henrietta's where he repeated the performance from the previous evening.

He decided to make the journey down to the town and find out if anyone knew of her whereabouts. She could be staying with someone down there just to avoid him.

He saddled his horse and began his ride. A half hour later, he hitched it to a railing outside of the grocer. The smells of the waterfront overwhelmed him, like they always did these days. The fresh salt air, tainted with the strong odor of fish, reminded him of what he'd given up.

The men working the docks cursed loud and incessantly. Mendleson found himself missing the companionship of those men. Of course, the men still working the docks and boats at this time of day were the lazy ones. The better fishermen had already put out to sea for the day. Paulus would be among them.

Mendleson stepped out of the cacophony and into the grocer, who had just opened for the day. The door, when it shut behind him, blocked out most of the noise.

"Mendleson," said a rotund man who stood behind the counter. "I don't see you much these days."

"How are you, Hugh? I don't have much need to come by."

"The farming must be treating you well."

"I'm not hurting for food, though I could use help harvesting it."

Hugh laughed. "What brings you here?"

Mendleson stepped up to the counter. "What can you tell me about Henrietta Swooth?"

"Why would I know more than you? You live across the way from her."

"She buys her groceries from you, Hugh."

Hugh nodded, causing his jowls to shake. "She does buy groceries from me. My boy delivered her order yesterday, as a matter of fact."

"I saw. They sat on her front porch, and were still there when I woke this morning. She doesn't answer her door."

"Well, now. That's odd."

"Why is that odd?"

"She sent a note with my boy, asking for me to send for a coach."

"A coach? Did she leave already?"

Hugh squinted. "Why the sudden interest?"

"We talked the other night at the festival."

Hugh smiled. "Finally, though I'm not sure why you'd pick her."

"No, it's not what you think. I said something. I'm not sure what, and she left, offended. I only want to apologize."

"That woman is a bit odd. My wife swears by her viewings, though, and she pays on time."

Mendleson wanted to reach out and slap the grocer. "Did she leave already?"

"What? Oh, why, no. There's not a coach due for another two days."

Mendleson slapped the counter.

"Why are you so upset?"

Mendleson couldn't tell Hugh about the dream. It hardly made sense to Mendleson. "I just want to make sure she's all right. I just want to apologize. Look, thanks for your help, Hugh. Tell your wife I said hello."

"It was good to see you down here. I'm sure everything is all right."

Mendleson left and went in search of the Justice. He'd want the man with him when he entered Henrietta's home. He couldn't keep the thought that she was in trouble out of his head.

‡

"When will that man get the hint and leave me alone?" Henrietta asked her empty room when she saw Mendleson approach her house through the crack in the shades. This time, he had the Justice with him.

For a moment, her heart warmed. It seemed obvious he was worried about her, but when she thought about her vision it only made her more frustrated. *How can I get rid of him?* His concern would result in his death. She couldn't allow that.

Whatever she wanted, she couldn't let him find her now. *Time to hide.*

She went to the rear of her little home and pulled up the cellar door. She climbed down into the hole, the darkness of her cellar swallowing her up. She could only hope they wouldn't be too thorough in their search.

She worked herself into a corner, out of the way of the light that would poor through the cellar door when they eventually opened it. *I hope there aren't too many spiders down here.*

She heard the door above open, and then the shades. She could tell light flooded the room above as little rays poked down through the floorboards, illuminating the dust that came free with every step the two men made.

A thump landed on the table. *Maybe they brought the groceries in.*

"Well, it looks like you're right, Mendleson. Something certainly happened to her. Are you sure she didn't just go to visit someone?"

"I'm pretty sure," said Mendleson. "Hugh said his delivery boy brought a message from her. How could he have done that if she wasn't here? Why wouldn't she bring in her groceries?"

"What did the message say again?"

"She asked for him to send for a coach."

"Maybe the coach arrived already," said the Justice.

"It didn't. Hugh said there wouldn't be another coach for two days."

Two days? I have to pretend to be somewhere else for another two days? She wanted to curse, but held her breath instead. *I can wait two days.*

"Curious. You didn't have anything to do with her disappearance, did you?"

"Why would I?" Mendleson said. His voice sounded indignant to Henrietta's ears. "Why would I come and get you to search for her if I had something to do with it?"

"I just have to ask."

The Justice walked to the rear of her home where the cellar door was. The door opened, and Henrietta crouched down, trying to make herself as small as possible. She hid her face in her dress.

"Is there a lamp in here?" the Justice asked.

She heard Mendleson moving around in an apparent search for something. He stopped. "How about a candle?"

"That will work."

Mendleson moved to the cellar door with the Justice. The Justice lowered his hand into the room, followed by his head. He apparently didn't want to climb down. Henrietta prayed he wouldn't change his mind and kept herself as still as she could. She also prayed he would hurry. Her legs were starting to cramp.

After a few moments, the Justice withdrew, taking the candle with him. The door shut. "She's not down there."

"Then where is she?" Mendleson asked. She could hear the confusion in his voice. It was mixed with something else. Anguish?

It didn't matter so much as long as he remained safe and ignorant of where she was.

The two men milled around a bit longer before eventually leaving.

Henrietta stood, rubbing cramps out of her legs. "Two days," she said softly.

She climbed out of the cellar and shut the door behind her. She brushed herself off, then looked at the table. On it, her groceries waited.

"I can do it," she said. "I can wait two days."

THREE

The next day, Mendleson made sure the work he did on his farm kept him in sight of Henrietta's house. He felt sure she was still there. He couldn't explain it, even to himself.

He also couldn't explain why, of a sudden, he felt so obsessed with her. They hadn't spoken a word to each other before the festival. The way she left their conversation, and her complete absence since, certainly seemed to indicate she had little desire to speak to him again.

"It's only because I want to apologize," he said to himself as he dug at a particularly persistent weed. The weed had become a frustrating metaphor for his obsession with the Seer.

He pulled on the weed, putting his weight behind it. After a brief struggle, the root of the weed finally gave up and pulled free, depositing Mendleson on his back.

"Great," he said, then sat up and tossed the weed into the waiting cart.

He looked across the way again. Henrietta's home hadn't changed since the last time he looked.

"One thing I can thank you for," he said. "I haven't dreamed of the fire the last two nights."

No. Instead, I've got this other dream. He thought back to the night of sleep he'd had, again interrupted by a dream of something dark coming for her. He couldn't shake the feeling Henrietta was in danger.

What really irked him was that the Justice seemed to think there was little amiss. There weren't any signs of distress in her house. There was nothing to indicate she hadn't just gone somewhere for the day, other than the message from her to the grocer, and the Justice dismissed that.

Whatever help she needed, and Mendleson felt sure she needed help, he decided he would be the one that would have to give it to her. He was not about to let Henrietta's house burn with her inside it.

As evening approached, he was growing tired of watching. He still refused to stop, but he was beginning to think that maybe she had left for good without the coach she had requested.

He stabled the horse and went inside to make his evening meal. A quarter loaf of bread and vegetable stew. He didn't even heat the stew that long. He wanted to get back to his watch.

He dug out the center of the bread, forming a bowl, and poured in the stew. He grabbed a spoon and took the whole thing out to his front steps to sit and eat.

Dusk had come while he prepared the meal. He dipped the excess bread into the stew and took a bite. It wasn't all that warm, but he didn't care.

A lone tree in Henrietta's garden blocked his view of her door, but he could see the window.

At first, he couldn't place what was different about the window. In the near dark, it was hard to discern details.

But after a moment, he figured it out. *Her shades are closed.* The Justice had opened them when they went into the house. *Were they closed all day? Or just now?* He thought back over the day, but couldn't remember. He thought maybe they had been shut all day, but he somehow hadn't noticed until now.

Or she came home and shut them while I was cooking.

It didn't matter really when it happened. What it meant was that she was still around.

He set his meal down on the step and stood up. *I'm just going over there to apologize.* But in his heart, he knew there was more. He wanted to make sure she was alright, that she wasn't in danger.

Just after his first step, he caught the flicker of a dim light as it escaped from behind the shades. *She's home.* He picked up his pace.

As he approached the road, a cold breeze came from the north, carrying an almost wintery chill. He shivered. The breeze carried a sound with it. Horses.

Mendleson stopped and crouched down behind a

large stone that had marked his property for as long as he could remember. No man or horse could move it.

He had no idea why he hid. The breeze, the sound of the horses. It didn't feel right, and he heeded his feelings.

Moments later, a quartet of horses rode down the lane pulling a coach behind them. The coach, painted black, seemed over-large and sinister. Lamps on either side of the driver's bench illuminated the area around it. The driver was just a big black shape, a shadow.

Something about it frightened Mendleson, and he wished for it to pass on by. But he knew it wouldn't.

It pulled to a stop in front of Henrietta's home in a rush of noise and scattering dust blown by the breeze.

The driver climbed down, took a step toward Henrietta's home, then stopped and looked back at Mendleson.

It knows I'm here. He ducked behind the rock. *I'm not here, I'm not here.*

Tense moments passed while he imagined it coming for him, imagined it reaching out and grasping his forehead and crushing it.

He heard it turn, and take steps away from him.

He knew what it was. It was the thing in his dream, and it wasn't here for him. *It's here for Henrietta.*

‡

When Henrietta closed her shades early in the morning, she knew she would be taking a risk, but it was less of a risk than having someone see her through her window. And she certainly didn't want to remain stuck hiding in the cellar the whole day.

"Two days for a coach," she said. "Unbelievable."

But there was nothing for it. If she had to wait, she had to wait, and hide.

She spent the day going through her things a little more carefully than she had the day before. She had time.

She set the things she wanted to take out on the table. Figurines, little pieces of artwork, letters, books, clothes. Anything she couldn't bear to part with. By mid-morning, the pile had begun to spill off the table, and she realized it wouldn't do. She couldn't take everything, even if she wanted to.

She went to the window and peeked through the shades. Mendleson was out working his farm, near the road. A little excitement flowed through her. She knew exactly what he was doing, and it made her happy enough for a moment that she smiled.

She scolded herself. "You know what will happen to him if you don't get rid of him, Henrietta. Forget about him."

But she couldn't. It didn't hurt that she liked to look at him. He was a strong man, kept his thick hair cropped short. The pain of his tragedy was written on his face, but she remembered when he smiled while talking to her at the festival. *I can't let him do that again, or I'll never want him to leave.*

"Henrietta, stop thinking about him and get to work."

She forced herself to leave the window and go back to sorting what she would take with her.

She started with her needs. Clothes. Her tools she used to See. She didn't really need those, she knew. They were mostly props, and not actually necessary to See. Where she was going, she didn't think she would need them. *But one never knows.* Besides, the ball, eight inches round and pure crystal, had belonged to her grandmother. She couldn't part with it.

Once those were in, she still had room left, so she began adding her books and other things. A comb her mother had given her. A beautiful figurine of the sea goddess given to her by a woman she'd helped to avoid a terrible fate. Henrietta couldn't remember what the fate was, but she adored the figurine.

She examined her trunk, and then sat in a chair.

"Who am I fooling?" she asked herself. "I'll be dead in a month or two. I won't need any of this stuff."

But she couldn't part with it.

Her work was done. Now, all she had to do was wait for the coach. Then she could leave, and Mendleson would be safe from sharing her fate.

She went back to the window to watch him.

When she saw him, her heart caught again, like it seemed to do ever since their conversation. "I didn't mean to put you in danger when I came here," she said as if he could hear her. "I was only trying to escape my fate. I only wanted to live as long as my grandmother.

"Of course, I should have realized I couldn't escape it."

She sighed, then went and sat in her reading chair. She stared at the trunk and tried to decide where to have the coachman take her once he finally arrived. The only destination she could settle on, however, was *away*.

When she woke from her inadvertent nap, she realized it was almost evening. She cut the wick on a candle short, then lit it. She hoped the little bit of light wouldn't leak through her shades too much.

Her stomach growled. She hadn't eaten since morning. She went through the groceries, and pulled out a loaf of bread and the smoked pork. She couldn't afford to cook and have the fire signal that someone was home.

The pork tasted salty, more than she usually preferred. If she were staying, she'd have a talk with Hugh about it, but for now, she had little choice.

"I hope that coachman arrives in the morning. I don't want to have to sit in here another whole..."

A knock at the door interrupted her monologue. She blew out the candle, hoping it wasn't too late.

She went to the window and peered through it. On the side of the road, she saw a big, black coach, lit by lamps at each corner. Her fear that Mendleson discovered her subsided. The coach had arrived early.

"Time to leave."

She went to the trunk and shut it, then dragged it to the door.

Henrietta opened the door, and then she stood, frozen. It was not a coachman at her door. What stood at the door was the stuff of her nightmares, the stuff of her visions.

Her fate stood two heads taller than her, a black cowl hiding a face that wasn't a face. It had no eyes. She thought she could make out a mouth among the shadows.

Its lips moved. A raspy sound came out. "It is time," it said.

"No," she whispered.

The thing's arm shot out and grabbed her by the throat. Sharp talons tipped its fingers and dug into her flesh. She could not move for fear of having her throat ripped out.

"It is time."

The wraith, for that's what it had to be, brought its other arm up to her face and toward her eyes.

‡

Without thinking about what he was doing, Mendleson reached down and dug a fairly large stone from the ground. When it came free, he hefted it a couple times and decided it would do. For a moment, he wished he had a real weapon, a sword or something. But the stone was all he had. *I'm no swordsman, anyway.*

He peeked out from his hiding place behind the monstrous rock. The shadow man moved with a measured gait toward Henrietta's front door. It was not looking at him. The horses were calm and reserved.

I hope they stay that way.

He moved out from his hiding place. Making as little noise as possible, he snuck across the road while keeping the horses between him and the shadowy figure. The horses looked at him, but did not grow agitated by his presence.

He snuck around to the back of the coach and peeked around it. The shadow man had just passed Henrietta's tree. Mendleson waited for it to move a little further along before stepping out from his hiding place.

He worked even harder at being quiet. He didn't know why, but he had a feeling if the shadow man turned around on him, he might not live through the experience.

The cold breeze picked up a little as he moved, making him shiver.

The thing was almost at her door. *I have to make it to the tree. Quiet, Mendleson. Quiet.*

Step after step, he moved closer to the tree. It blocked his view of the window, but not his view of the shadow man. A couple more steps.

Then he was behind the tree, hidden from the shadow man. Maybe fifteen paces from Henrietta's door. Close enough to help her, but far enough away to go unnoticed if she didn't need his help.

The shadow man knocked at the door. Its rap, rap, rap sounded distant in the strange, unseasonably-cold breeze.

It waited. Mendleson waited while watching from behind the tree. His muscles felt tight with anticipation. He hadn't seen Henrietta in two days. He needed to see her, but he feared for her. He feared this man.

Why am I waiting? Why don't I just rush him?

He answered himself. *Because he might only be a coach driver arrived early.*

His argument sounded hollow.

The door opened, and he saw Henrietta, her face illuminated by a candle that she held. His heart thumped in his chest. The candle light made her beauty even more manifest.

For a moment, he thought everything would be all right. He thought that it was the coach driver, come to take her where she wanted to go, and his heart fell. He wouldn't get the chance to see her again.

Then her eyes went wide, and the same look of horror that he'd seen at the festival crossed her face again.

Mendleson heard the shadow man speak, a raspy sort of voice, like bones grinding together. "It is time."

He couldn't hear Henrietta's reply, but her lips shaped the word, "No."

The man's arm reached out and grabbed her throat.

Mendleson launched himself into a run, holding the rock up high. *I'm too late! He's going to kill her before I get there!*

But the shadow man didn't seem to be choking her, not yet. It was just holding her in place. It brought its other arm up and moved it toward her face.

Mendleson raced as fast as he could. Just as he arrived at the shadow man, he brought the rock down with both hands, smashing it into his skull. The skull caved in, almost as if it hadn't been completely solid, and then Mendleson's body collided with the shadow man, knocking them both sprawling.

The shadow man's arm came free of Henrietta and grasped at Mendleson. It had sharp fingernails. Knives on the end of its fingers. They dug at his flesh, but Mendleson didn't care. He brought the rock down again on the man's head.

The claws dug deeper.

Again, he brought the rock down. The shadow man shuddered, and then relaxed its grip on him. The claws came loose.

Mendleson could feel drips of blood on his skin where the claws had penetrated. He paid them no mind.

Excitement rushed through him, the brief fight energizing him. He brought the rock down once again, just to be sure.

He pushed himself up, then stood over the shadow man. Its hood had come free, and for the first time, he saw one of the thing's hands.

It hadn't been a man, not at all.

His chest felt tight, and it grew harder to breathe.

He backed away from the creature, stumbling over one of its outstretched legs.

He didn't fall to the ground. A pair of arms caught him. Henrietta's.

"What is that?" he asked, short of breath.

FOUR

Henrietta stood for a moment, trying to take in what happened. The wraith was the easy part. It had come for her, like she knew it would. She just hadn't imagined it would be so soon.

She hadn't expected to be saved. Not from a wraith. And not by Mendleson, of all people. She didn't know where he had come from, as she'd only had eyes for the wraith as it held her in place and brought its terrible claws toward her eyes.

A rock had come down while she waited for the end, driven by a pair of hands, and smashed the wraith's skull. It fell away, its claws ripping at the flesh of her neck. She felt at her neck, felt the scrape marks. They stung, but she didn't feel the blood she expected.

Of course, she couldn't die here. Or, at least, the chances of it were not great. Her death would happen someplace else.

Rage had overcome Mendleson. He smashed at the wraith again and again until at last, he tried to stand.

He did stand, for a moment, before she saw that he was falling backward, toward her. On instinct, she reached out and caught him, kept him from falling to the stone pathway.

It left her view open, and she could see past him, to the open cowl, where it was obvious her attacker was not a man. *He must not have realized what he was saving me from.*

She held him up until he caught himself and got his own feet under him.

"What... what is that?" he asked.

Once Mendleson had control of himself, she let go. "It's a wraith."

"A wraith?"

She nodded. She didn't want to go into it here. *I have to leave.* She looked out to the road and saw the coach sitting there, waiting for her.

"I have to go."

She went back into her house to get her trunk.

"Where are you going?" Mendleson asked. He moved to help her with the trunk.

"I don't know. I can't stay here, though."

Together, they brought the trunk out to the coach and strapped it on to the rack. She was grateful for the help.

"Why not?"

"The wraith. It will come for me until I'm dead."

"But it's dead. I killed it."

She shook her head. "No, you didn't. It can't be killed. It will wake and come after me. I don't know how much time I have left."

She looked back at her home. "I'm going to miss this place," she said. *The way the sun sets on the horizon, my tree, my garden, the quiet.* "You've been a good neighbor, Mendleson. Go hide in your home and don't come out until morning."

She climbed up into the driver's seat.

"I could come with you."

Her vision came back to her, and terror leaped into her chest fully formed. "No! You can't do that."

"Why not?"

"Just go home. Thank you for your help, but please. Go home and hide."

He pulled the coach door open and jumped inside.

"I'm not going home until I know why you were so afraid of me the other night," he said. "I didn't mean to scare you."

"You didn't scare me. I..." Movement by her house caught her eye and interrupted her thought.

The wraith was trying to stand. *Too late. I can still drop him off later. I can still change it.*

"Shut the door, Mendleson."

"What?"

"Shut the door! It's waking up."

It had pushed itself to its knees. She assumed it had

knees. She didn't really know what they were beyond what she had gathered from stories heard at her grandmother's feet.

She heard the door shut, and she urged the horses into motion. For a moment, she worried they wouldn't accept her, that they were some sort of ethereal creatures.

But they moved, and the coach lurched and picked up speed. *Just horses.*

‡

For what felt like half the night, Mendleson rattled around inside the cabin of the coach while Henrietta drove the horses as hard as she could. It gave him time to think and reflect, but like the bumpy ride, his thoughts were disjointed and disconnected.

The interior of the coach seemed far more luxurious in the dark than he would have imagined a hired coach would be. The walls were embossed in leather, and the seat felt well cushioned. If Henrietta hadn't driven the horses so hard, it might have been a really nice ride as far as coach travel went.

Once inside and they were on their way, he thought for a while about what that thing was. He'd never seen the like, but he suspected few people ever had. That Henrietta knew about it, knew it wouldn't die, that scared him. *Has she seen them before? Is that why she moved here in the first place? Did she know it was coming?*

Of course, they weren't questions he could answer on his own. He'd somehow have to convince her to answer them if he was to protect her.

His mind went quiet for a moment.

I am going to protect her. He knew it.

He tried to argue against himself. *What about that thing? How are you going to protect her if you can't kill it? How are you supposed to fight something that won't die?*

He didn't know the answers. But the answers didn't matter. She needed his help, and he wouldn't fail her. *I'll find a way.*

An hour or so later, he looked out the window on his right to find the moon had risen. In the near distance, he could see it reflecting off water. The Western Sea. She'd driven them down through the town and south along the Coast Road.

He tried to think of where they might be, how close to the next town, and realized they wouldn't reach it for hours yet. *How long have we been running?*

He opened the side window. The salt air spilled into the cabin. Whatever chill had come with the wraith was gone. The coolness of the air now came from the sea.

"Henrietta!" he yelled.

She didn't respond, so he repeated his call.

"What?"

"You need to slow down! You'll kill the horses!"

He didn't hear an answer, but after a minute or so,

he could tell she'd eased up. The coach slowed, the ride grew smoother.

After a few minutes, he leaned out the window again. "Stop the coach," he said. "I need to talk to you."

"We need to keep moving."

"It's got to be miles behind us by now. It can't travel that fast, can it?"

Several moments passed before he heard an answer. "I don't know."

"Then just stop long enough so I can climb up next to you. I think we really need to talk."

"Fine."

The coach slowed to a stop, and Mendleson stepped out and shut the door. He climbed up to sit on the bench next to her. As soon as he was sitting, she got the horses moving again.

"So what do we need to talk about?"

"Where are we going?"

"South."

"I know that."

"I don't know where I'm going. I'm just running."

He tried to get a look into her eyes, but she turned away from him. "Why are you running? Why was it trying to kill you?"

She didn't answer.

"If I'm going to help, I need to know what's going on."

She did turn to look at him then. Moonlight reflected off her eyes, but he couldn't tell whether he saw anger or tears. "You are not going to help me. I can't allow that to happen."

"What?"

"You're getting off in the next town, and we'll never see each other again."

‡

Mendleson looked upset, but Henrietta didn't care. She could not have his death on her hands.

"What do you mean we'll never see each other again? You need me."

Henrietta hated sitting next to him, hated having this conversation. None of the women had ever questioned her insight. *Of course, Mendleson doesn't know why I'm trying to rid myself of him.*

She looked deep into his eyes, lit as they were by the lamps that burned on the side of the coach. The worry she saw there made her wonder. She surprised herself by wondering aloud.

"You're not trying to help me because of your wife, are you?" she asked.

He sat back and looked away. She tried to guess what he was thinking, but could not conjure anything specific.

"No," he said. "I don't think so. I'm not sure."

He turned back to her, and she did see tears in his eyes. She hadn't meant to hurt him. She hadn't realized how vulnerable he was to thoughts of his wife.

She opened her mouth to say something, but words wouldn't form. *I'm sorry?* It seemed too little.

"You were home the other day when I came by and knocked on the door," he said.

She nodded. No point in lying to him now.

"I only wanted to apologize for whatever it was that I did to frighten you."

She looked ahead, pretending to watch the road ahead. "You didn't frighten me."

"But you looked so scared after I touched your hand. I thought for sure..."

"You didn't frighten me." *Why won't I tell him? He knows what I am.* The only answer she could come up with was that she didn't really want him to go. But she did want him to go. She felt certain of it. She wouldn't allow herself to be responsible for his death.

"If I didn't frighten you, then what happened? Why did you hide from me?"

She decided she'd tell him, in the hope it would frighten him away. She turned to face him again. He looked so earnest.

"When our hands touched, I had a vision." she said.

"A vision?"

She didn't want to talk about it. It was too close to the vision of her own death that she had when she received the sight. She'd had it drilled into her that she should never reveal that vision. But here she was, about to reveal it to a man she hardly knew. A thought came to her.

"I saw you with me, and I saw you die," she said. She felt proud of having told him of his part in her vision without revealing the whole thing.

"How do I die?" he asked. He didn't seem afraid at all.

"Wraiths, in the mountains."

He appeared to think for a moment. She liked watching him think. He may have been a fisherman once, but he wasn't one of those that frequented the taverns along the waterfront.

"You were afraid for me," he said. "You think that if I stay with you, I'll die."

"You will die. I saw it."

"But you told me at the festival that your visions don't always come true. You implied that they can be worked around."

"I did say that," she said. "And that's why I want you to leave. It's the easiest way to work around it."

He reached out to her. "But if I leave, you'll die."

She shied away from him. He seemed to realize what he'd done and let his hand drop.

"I'll die, anyway, Mendleson. It can't be helped. I've known from the day I received the Sight how my end would come."

"That's horrid."

She shook her head. "It is the way of things. I wish it could be different. I wish I had more time, but knowing my end is the price of the gift. There is no way I can escape it."

"There's got to be a way. If I can avoid the fate you've seen for me by just leaving you, then you should be able to avoid yours by just never going where you saw your end."

"Mendleson, it doesn't work that way. For me, the threads of fate will be constructed in such a way as to place me where I need to be. There is another Seer coming into the world, and she needs my Sight."

Henrietta couldn't believe how comfortable with the whole thing she was making herself sound. It frightened her to her core.

"But..."

She cut him off. "No. I already tried to circumvent my fate. I came here, and in doing so, I tied you to me. You were never in my visions before."

They rode in silence for a while. She stole glances at him as often as she dared, but he looked out to sea.

I wonder if he misses the sea? I don't have the right to take the possibility of returning from him.

The road began to curve, following the coastline, to the south east. More and more trees sprouted up to her left, high on the hills. They were leaving the more arid lands to the north. And she was getting tired. She'd been awake since the sun had risen.

"Henrietta," Mendleson said, causing her to jump a little in her seat.

"What?"

"I dreamed of that wraith the last two nights."

She jerked her head over to look at him. "You what?"

"I dreamed of that wraith, or something much like it each night since we touched at the festival. I knew it was coming for you. What does that mean?"

"I don't know. I've never heard of such a thing. Tell me about it."

"It was just a dream. I don't remember a whole lot about it except that wraith, it had to be the wraith, was chasing after you. I was chasing after you, too."

She thought about it for a moment. *Is it possible? Did some of my vision spill over our connection?*

"You're right," she said. "It was just a dream."

"But it couldn't be just a dream. I dreamed of that thing, and then it showed up. That must mean something."

Finally, she gave up trying to reason with him. He obviously had no regard for his own safety. "Look, Mendleson. You are leaving me when we reach the next town. I will not be responsible for your death."

"You're not responsible for me. I'm not leaving."

"How can you be so stubborn?" She wanted to cry, but wouldn't let herself.

"Why are you in so much of a hurry to die? I can help protect you."

Then the tears did come. She couldn't stop them. "I'm not in a hurry. I just don't have a choice."

"Then I'm staying, at least until we come to this mountain where you see me die. If we're still alive, then I'll leave."

She wiped at her eyes, trying to clear the tears. She didn't know what to say. It might work as well if they waited until they reached the mountains before he left. As long as he never went to the plateau in the mountains where the monolith stood.

They wouldn't have long, but for the first time in her life, she'd met a man that didn't fear her, and she didn't want to let him go.

The coach rolled on in silence for a while, until he noticed her yawn.

"Give me the reins. I'll drive for awhile. You climb in the cabin and sleep."

"But..." Another yawn cut off her protest.

He stopped the coach and she climbed into the cabin and lay down on the seat. It didn't take her long to drift off into dreams, but not a one of them was sweet.

FIVE

Clouds hung around her, blocking her views of the other peaks. She looked out over an abyss from her perch on the edge of the plateau. Behind her, she knew, stood the monolith. She didn't have to turn around to know it was there. She could feel its energy reaching for her, beckoning her to come closer.

She knew she would give in, eventually, but she would put it off as long as she could. She'd seen this vision a hundred times. She knew how it ended.

But she felt something different. Another presence. An arm around her waist.

She looked to her left, and found Mendleson standing next to her, content, a smile on his face that held no hint of sadness.

She, too, felt content. This was how things should be.

No.

He turned to look at her. His sun-darkened face gave her hope for the first time.

No!

Something was wrong, though. She knew what was coming. Why was he so happy? Didn't he know?

She opened her mouth to tell him, but she couldn't. The words wouldn't leave her lips.

He leaned forward, taking her partly open mouth as an invitation, and kissed her. It was the first time. Her heart exploded in her chest.

And she started to cry. She knew it would be the last time.

She tried to push him away, but he held her tight, and in truth, she didn't want it to end. She wanted the kiss to last forever. She felt connected to him, a part of him.

No! Stop! Run away!

She felt them before she saw them. Wraiths. They had come for her.

She pushed Mendleson away and ran for the Monolith.

The wraiths appeared from the mist surrounding the mountain top. They circled around her and the monolith. The circle closed on her.

She was ready—and sad.

Mendleson stood, raced toward the wraiths. He swung a sword among them, knocking them down.

Run, Mendleson!

The wraiths turned away from her to deal with the threat. They converged on him, ignoring the sword. There were so many, she couldn't see him through their black cloaks.

They came away from him, and returned to circle her. Through the cracks in the circle, she could see him where he lay, prone, not breathing. Dead.

"Noooo!" Henrietta shouted, waking herself from the vision. Her heart beat rapidly in her chest, and her muscles were tense, ready to fight. Ready to fight for him.

"Are you alright?"

His voice comforted her. He was still with her, still alive. She looked to where she knew he had been sleeping. The moonlight pouring through the window showed he had propped himself up with an arm, and the blanket that was draped over him had slipped down to expose his chest. She had a fleeting desire to climb out of bed and put her fingertips on his chest. After the kiss... *Could it really be like that?*

She wanted to find out, but resisted. It would only make it harder to do what she knew she had to do.

"A bad dream," she said. "Go back to sleep."

"Right," he said, and continued to look at her for a bit, before resting his head on the blanket he had rolled up into a pillow.

In the dark, she couldn't see his eyes, but she imagined them looking at her like he had in the vision. She wanted him to look at her that way. Wanted to feel his lips on hers.

But the vision seemed clear. He would die if she remained with him. She couldn't let him continue on with her.

But how to make him go? *How do I escape him?*

They'd driven the coach hard through the night, taking turns resting. It hadn't been nearly as good as a real sleep, but it kept them going.

It was near morning when they reached the town. They had argued again when she told him he should leave. He refused, again arguing that they were nowhere near the mountain she saw in her vision, so there was little danger for him.

Once she had given up arguing with him, they decided to continue on through the day and get as far as they could from the wraith. He suggested it might look for her in the next town. She thought it might not matter where she was, but didn't push it. Distance might help.

So they continued on through the day, passing through a couple smaller coastal towns until they came to a significantly larger town that had more than one inn.

The only money they had on them was hers, and it wasn't a lot. They decided to share a room to conserve her money, and when they entered the room, he immediately took two blankets and made a place for himself to sleep on the floor.

Where his breath had now slipped back into an even, quiet rhythm.

She waited a bit longer, making sure he had fallen asleep. While she waited, her thoughts drifted back to the vision, and how it had changed since she'd first had it as a little girl.

It had frightened her, then. It brought her awake, crying. But back then, it was only her, surrounded by the wraiths. She didn't even remember the monolith appearing in that early vision.

She had talked with her grandmother about it. Her grandmother had seemed both joyous and sad at the same time, and Henrietta had picked up on it.

"Why are you both happy and sad, Gran?" Henrietta had asked.

"Ah, Henrietta, so perceptive. I am happy because you are like me, a Seer. You will know the ways of things before they come to pass."

"But why are you sad?"

Her grandmother had bent down then, and hugged her while whispering into her ear. "I am sad because you have seen the end of your days, as it is with all Seers. Do not tell others, as this vision is yours alone. Others will not understand."

"Is it a long time away?" she had asked, suddenly more frightened than when she thought it was just a dream.

"I cannot tell you. Your time is your time, and it is given only to you to know."

"Gran, do you know when you will die?" Henrietta had asked, then.

Gran had pulled away from her, and looked her in the eye. There were tears dripping down her weathered cheeks. "I do, child," she had said. "I have known since I was about your age."

Mendleson rolled over underneath his blankets and broke her out of her reverie. She had thought then that she would live as long as Gran, for her vision of herself had seemed so much older. She hadn't understood, when she was six, how quickly time sped along.

Henrietta forced herself out of bed and put her feet to the floor as gently as she could. She didn't want to wake him.

She looked at her trunk, which Mendleson had carried up the stairs on his own. *There's no way I'm carrying that back down.* She'd have to leave most of her things here, but her time felt so close, she didn't think she'd need them anymore.

She opened it, and one of the hinges squealed. She looked at Mendleson, fearing she'd wake him again, but he didn't move. *Thank the Fates.*

She dug through the trunk and pulled out two sets of clothes. She also withdrew her purse. She removed enough money from the purse for Mendleson to pay for breakfast and a ride home, and put the it next to the wash basin. He wouldn't need any for the room. The proprietor of the inn had required them to pay for that up front.

She took the pillowcase off her pillow and stuffed one change of clothes into it. She changed into the other, a violet dress that fit her well, but was loose enough to allow her to run. The money purse, she stowed in one of the dress' inner pockets.

She looked through the rest of her possessions, and could not think of another item that she must take with her. Then she looked at Mendleson.

A desire to kiss him for real flared up within her, but she tamped it down. She couldn't afford to have him wake. She couldn't afford to tie him to her further. It wasn't fair to him.

She picked up the stuffed pillow case from the bed, turned one last time to Mendleson, and whispered, "Thank you."

She opened the door, and stepped out into the hallway, closing the door behind her as gently as she could.

She shivered. The hallway felt cool, colder than she would have expected.

She turned down the hallway, took three steps, looked up, screamed.

‡

Mendleson didn't dream like he'd grown used to over the past four years. His dreams were blissfully free of the fire, of finding his wife and child crushed and burnt under the center beam. Neither did he dream of the dark thing coming to kill Henrietta.

Instead, he dreamed of Henrietta in his arms, he dreamed of holding her tight, caressing her hair. He dreamed he was the wall between her and a world that wanted to take her away from him.

Until she screamed and jolted him from his sleep.

"Are you all right?" he asked, turning to look at her. She was sitting up in the bed she had to herself.

He had thought about sharing the bed with her, when they first saw the room. It was large enough. But he decided against it. He hadn't wanted to give her another reason to argue with him about whether he would stay or go.

"A bad dream," she said. "Go back to sleep."

"Right," he said. He watched her for a moment, hoping she might say more. But when she didn't say anything else, he put his head back down on the rolled up blanket that served as a pillow and tried to go back to sleep.

When sleep finally came again, his dreams had changed. The dream of the dark thing, the wraith, had come back. The wraith chased Henrietta, and Mendleson couldn't catch it. He couldn't stop it. He raced as hard as he could, but it was faster. He caught up with her, and Henrietta turned and screamed.

Mendleson woke again, breathing hard. He looked up at the bed, wanting to reassure himself that Henrietta was safe, but the bed was empty. Out of the corner of his eye, he saw her trunk. It stood open.

He heard her scream again. *Not a dream.*

He jumped up and ran for the door, shedding the blankets as he went. He ripped open the door and looked down the hallway. A lamp at the end of the hall lit Henrietta and her attacker enough so that he could see the wraith.

It had Henrietta on her knees, its left hand about her throat. Its right hand hovered above her head, separated only by a couple inches and a ghostly light.

Mendleson didn't stop to wonder what it was doing to her.

"Leave her alone!" he yelled, and launched himself at the wraith.

The wraith looked up just as Mendleson crashed into it, and the two of them fell to the floor. The wraith plunged its claws into his side. Mendleson could feel the fire of them, but he ignored the fire, and punched it in the face as best he could.

It felt like punching mud. Every strike sunk in, but didn't seem to do much damage. The wraith struggled under him and tried to free itself. It disengaged its claws from his torso and tried to bring them up to his neck.

Mendleson caught them and pinned them to the floor before they could tear out his throat.

The two of them were stuck there for a moment, neither having an advantage they could press. Mendleson stared into its face for a moment, but in the near dark, he could see little of its features.

He looked for Henrietta, hoping she might be able to help him, but he saw her shadow slumped on the floor.

Rage and loss overcame him. "Not again!" he yelled. He looked up, saw the blackness of the stairwell. He kicked himself over, pulling the wraith with him, and threw the wraith down the stairs in one motion. He followed it down as fast as he could, taking the steps three at a time in the near dark, and slamming into the wraith at the bottom.

He threw the wraith out into the common room, which was mercifully empty of patrons. Mendleson picked up a chair, and was about to swing it at the wraith when the wraith came at him in a rush of cloak and shadow.

It knocked him down, and he dropped the chair. It reached for his throat, but Mendleson kicked out again, throwing the thing off him.

How do I end this?

They both got to their feet, and Mendleson found himself circling the wraith.

"You won't have her."

It hissed at him. "You can't thwart fate."

Their circling brought the wraith in front of the fireplace. The low glow from the still hot coals gave the wraith an orange aura. It also gave Mendleson an idea.

"I can certainly try," he said, then rushed the wraith.

It stuck its arms out, claws extended. Mendleson crashed into it, shoving it back. He ignored the arms and just kept pushing it backward, backward, and into the open fireplace.

Its cloak caught fire immediately, exploding in a huge burst, encasing the wraith in flame. It let out a high pitched wail that hurt Mendleson's ears. It spun around, trying to put out the flames but it was already too late.

The wraith dropped to the ground and writhed in decreasing movements until all that was left was a burning mass.

A man rushed forward carrying a bucket of water, and in the orange light, Mendleson recognized the innkeeper.

The innkeeper doused the flaming mass with water, and the fire went out. He stamped on it with his foot, extinguishing the last of the flames, then turned to confront Mendleson.

"What in the Seven Hells was that?"

"It's a..." He remembered Henrietta. "Henrietta!"

Mendleson pushed the innkeeper aside and rushed up the stairs.

Henrietta still lay slumped on the floor. He rolled her over so that she lay face up and saw that her chest still moved as she breathed. In the dim light, it was hard to tell, but her face looked pale.

He ran back to the room, found his shirt and put it on, ignoring the blood that dripped from the rents in his skin. He found the money she had left for him, and pocketed it. "You won't be free of me that easily," he said under his breath as he went back into the hall.

He bent down, and picked her up, slinging her over his shoulder. "I'm glad you're not very heavy," he said.

He picked up the pillowcase that held her belongings and went down the stairs.

At the bottom, the innkeeper confronted him again.

"You owe me for the damage in there," he said, pointing to the common room.

Mendleson dug into his pocket and selected a coin at random. He didn't want to argue, and he needed information. He held the coin up. "Tell me where I can find a healer."

The innkeeper looked at the coin for a second, then rose up on his toes. "That's hardly enough."

"We can stand here arguing about whether it's enough, or you can tell me where a healer is and take the money. I don't know if that thing has friends."

The innkeeper looked at him for a moment before worry overcame him. His eye twitched, and he jerked his head to look at his common room, then back to look at the coin.

"Fine," he said, and reached out for the coin.

Mendleson held it out of his reach. "The healer?" He wished he felt up to punching the man for wasting his time. As light as Henrietta was, he couldn't carry her forever. Especially not with his blood leaking all over.

"Down the South road on the left. Her name is Gretta."

"Thank you," Mendleson said, and dropped the coin into the man's outstretched hand.

He carried Henrietta out to the stable and found the horses, but they'd been unhitched from the coach.

He didn't think he had time to get the coach ready to go, so he draped Henrietta over the back of one of the horses, then lead it out of the stable. He found the South road, and followed it. As he lead the horse, he grew more and more tired and a bit dizzy. He knew he was losing blood. He hoped he would manage to keep enough in him to find the healer.

A great deal of time passed, he thought, before he found the healer. His vision had grown blurry. He knocked on the door, then sat down to wait. He heard footsteps, and the door opened.

"Who's there?" he heard a female voice say. "Oh, I see."

She reached down and pulled him up. "You've been in some trouble," she said.

Mendleson couldn't respond. He was too tired.

"Brode! Brode! Come here, I need your help." Then quieter, to him, "Come on in, and we'll get you fixed right up."

SIX

Henrietta's eyelids flipped open and she found herself staring up at a ceiling that looked familiar.

"So, Henrietta, it seems you've found a savior."

She absolutely recognized the voice. "Gretta."

Henrietta brought her elbows underneath her and pushed herself up. The room was exactly as she remembered it. When she looked at Gretta, she found the older woman hadn't changed much either. Her hair still hung straight and shoulder length, though there was a little more silver above her ears. Her smile was as welcoming as ever.

"How is it that you didn't come stay with me instead of at that awful inn that Rupert runs?"

"You know the innkeeper?"

"Of course, dear. He sends me work at least twice a week. Can't seem to keep his customers from getting hurt. Now answer my question."

If there was one thing Henrietta remembered about

Gretta, it was that Gretta could badger information out of a stone. With her, it was usually easier to just spill the seeds. "I didn't want to bring my trouble on you."

Gretta laughed. "Nonsense. You didn't want me getting my fingers on that man of yours. He's something special."

Henrietta shook her head. "He's just a friend...Wait. Is he here?"

"He's in the other room, sleeping off the draught I gave him."

"Sleeping off the... Gretta. How did I get here?" Henrietta remembered a wraith coming for her. It had her in its grip. It was pulling something out of her. Then nothing. Her memory ended.

"Your friend brought you here, strapped across a horse. I'm not sure what happened to either of you. A knock on the head for you, perhaps, but he had gashes all over him, and he lost a lot of blood, I think. It must have been some fight."

Worry overcame her. "Is he alright? He's not..."

Gretta reached out and patted Henrietta's shoulder. "Don't you worry. He's fine. He's got me to look after him."

Henrietta relaxed. She wished she knew what had happened. But as long as he didn't die because of her.

"How long will he be out?"

"A few hours, I should imagine. Enough for the salves to do their work."

Henrietta tried to push herself up. "Time to leave, then," she said.

Gretta held her down. "Woah, not yet. Not until I know you're recovered from that knock on the head. Besides, like I said, your man won't be awake for hours."

"He's not my man," she said. *Why does it feel wrong to say that?*

"I think he would differ. He seemed far more concerned with you than with himself."

"He thinks he can save me," Henrietta said softly.

Gretta's eyes went wide at that and she sat on the edge of the bed. "It can't be your time, can it?"

Henrietta nodded. "I can't see beyond the summer."

Gretta leaned over and wrapped her arms around her. Henrietta closed her eyes and tried not to cry. She felt just like when Gran had wrapped her up as a child, before Gran's time had come.

"I can't believe the fates would be so cruel," Gretta said as she sat back up.

Henrietta shook her head. "They aren't cruel, Gretta. They just are. Every person, every living thing, has their part to play."

"But we can all change our part. You've told me as much yourself."

"Not us. Not me."

"I don't understand," said Gretta.

Henrietta took a breath. She'd been told by her Gran not to reveal the secrets to any who weren't Seers, but at the moment, she didn't care. She'd tried to accept what she knew would come, but Mendleson kept interfering.

There was an attraction between them that could perhaps grow into more, given enough time. The kiss in her vision. Is that all she would be allowed?

She needed help, and Gran was long dead.

"What my Gran told me is that there are a limited number of Seer's at any one time. Their gift is that they can see the possible futures. They can see the fate of people so that they might change it."

Gretta nodded, but did not speak.

"Gran told me there are two prices the Seer must pay for her Sight," Henrietta continued. "The first is that the Seer learns of her death on the day she receives the gift. The second..."

"The second is what?" Mendleson's voice came from the doorway.

Henrietta turned and saw him leaning against the door frame for support. His face looked whiter than normal, and he seemed a little wobbly. "Mendleson..."

Gretta said at the same time, "You should not be up."

"What is the second price, Henrietta?" he asked. As wobbly as his body was, his eyes were steady.

"Seer's can not change their fate."

Gretta stood up and went to Mendleson. She led him to the bed and forced him to sit. This allowed Henrietta a chance to study the man that brought her here.

He wasn't wearing a shirt, but with the number of bandages Gretta had applied, he didn't need one. He was more bandage than skin.

Once Gretta had him sitting, he asked, "Then what is it that I have done these last three days? Haven't I changed your fate?"

Henrietta didn't know what to say for a moment. He had changed her fate. Just talking to her on the festival night had changed it slightly. It put him in the middle of it. It changed his fate more than hers.

Or, was it the other way around? *Was it I that changed his fate? Am I responsible for this?*

"I wish I could talk to Gran." she said.

"Why?"

She hadn't realized she said it aloud. "She had more time to learn. She had more knowledge about the gift than anyone I knew."

"What would she know that you don't?" he asked.

"She would know whether you are correct. Did you change my fate already? Or is it I that changed your fate? Is the vision I had of your death due to my attempt to change my fate?"

His eyes grew soft with concern for her. "Don't you even think that. I didn't have to reach for you. I didn't have to follow after you. How could your vision of my death be your fault?"

"I came to your town to try to avoid my fate. I thought that if I stayed away from anywhere that remotely looked like my vision, I would be safe from it. Why is it that Gran got to live to be an old woman, yet I must die before I've even had a chance to live? I hate my gift."

The tears came. She hadn't meant to say that. She'd never told anyone how she felt. She had never before come close to saying it aloud. She'd kept it from herself for so many years.

Gretta bent down to give her a hug and comfort. "There, there," she said. "We'll figure this out."

Henrietta wished she believed her friend. She wished it was Mendleson that had put his arms around her.

‡

Mendleson felt awful. His head was woozy from either the tea the healer had dosed him with or the blood loss. He ached everywhere.

But it was good to see that Henrietta was awake and that she appeared to be much better off than he. He'd silently congratulated himself as he stood in the doorway, nearly falling over, for keeping her alive for another day.

Of course, he'd then made a fool of himself by practically falling onto the bed when Gretta had pulled him over. She apparently expected him to be asleep. He took a little pleasure in frustrating her.

He hadn't quite managed to follow all of the conversation, but he'd followed enough. He couldn't accept that she had put him in danger. *I made choices. My fate is my fault.*

He couldn't accept that he hadn't changed her fate.

If he hadn't stepped in, she would be dead now. Not sometime in the future.

When Gretta hugged Henrietta, Mendleson found himself wishing that it was he providing her comfort. Whatever she thought, he had made her his responsibility. Of course, he could barely keep upright at the moment.

"What's there to figure out?" Henrietta asked, after she pulled away from Gretta's embrace.

"Yes," Mendleson said, remembering the burning lump he'd left on the floor of the inn. "What is there to figure out? I killed that thing. I know I did."

"You can't kill them, Mendleson. I told you that."

"It was a burning lump when I left it. There was hardly anything left."

"Even if you did kill it," Henrietta said, "There are more than one. Another will be sent, if they aren't already on the way. That might not have even been the same one."

"Then what do we do? How do we change your fate?"

Henrietta pounded the bed. "By the Fates, Mendleson, don't you get it? My fate can't be changed! This," and she waved her arm around the room, "you sitting here hurt, this is all part of it. I'm not supposed to die in this town! I wasn't going to die that first time! You have to get away from me!"

He thought of another tack. "What if I can't?"

She calmed down a bit. "What do you mean?"

"What if I can't leave? What if I try? Won't something bring me back? What if it's too late?"

"How can that be? You just have to go."

"Really? Like you tried to do last night? Like you tried in Porthead?" Mendleson watched the color drain from her face. "Both times you've tried to leave me out of it, events conspired against you to bring me back into it. Did those wraiths show up to kill you, or to keep me with you?"

No one spoke while Henrietta digested what he said. He didn't believe it true, but he was sure she would. *I'll use anything I can in order to keep my promise.*

"Wouldn't it be safer for both of us," he said, "if you just accepted that I was coming with you while we figure out how to change your fate?"

"I'm so sorry, Mendleson. I never meant to do this to you."

"Why are you so sure it was your fault?" he asked.

"You were never in my vision of my end until that night at the festival."

He wanted to reach out and wipe the tear from her eye that he saw there. "I still don't believe that means it was your fault."

They fell back into silence again. Gretta stood between them, looking first at one, then the other, apparently waiting for something.

"Now that's settled," she said, "would you allow me to give you some advice, Henrietta?"

Henrietta nodded.

"I may not be a Seer, but I am an old woman who happens to be a healer. I've met quite a few people and learned quite a few things. I had the opportunity, once, to treat a man that was on his way to visit the Oracle of Arabeth."

"Who is that?" Mendleson asked.

"When he told me, I had no idea who he was talking about, either, so I asked him the same thing you just asked me."

"Arabeth is near my home, but I haven't heard of this Oracle," said Henrietta.

"He told me that a Seer in his village had told him to seek out the Oracle for an answer to his question. I can't do anything but imagine that this Oracle is a Seer."

"Henrietta," Mendleson said, "Maybe this Oracle could help us find a way to change your fate."

"What about your fate?" she asked. "Aren't you worried about it?"

"My fate, too," he lied. He wasn't worried about his fate at all. If he died saving her, it would be a fair price for his atonement.

"But, Arabeth," Henrietta said. "The mountains. We'd be traveling directly toward where my vision tells me I will end."

Mendleson hadn't realized that. "It seems there is little choice. We either continue as we have, fighting it all the way, and find ourselves forced there, or we choose to go and hope we find help before the end."

More silence followed as they mulled it over in their

heads. Eyes met, glances were exchanged. Mendleson hoped she'd decide soon. He wanted to lay down and go back to sleep.

"You're sure you want to do this?" Henrietta asked.

Mendleson nodded. "I'll fight to keep you alive as long as there is breath in me." It sounded silly to his ears, but he'd said it, and meant it.

"Will he be ready by tomorrow, Gretta?"

Mendleson didn't give Gretta a chance to answer. "I'll be ready."

Gretta sighed. "Then you'd better get back into your own bed and sleep off that tonic I gave you."

Mendleson tried to stand, and had to wait for help from Gretta.

"Tomorrow," he said as he left. "And don't try leaving without me. I can't fight another one of those things right now."

SEVEN

Henrietta felt much better now that she had confessed her weakness to Mendleson and Gretta. To have her fear and frustration out in the open seemed to have lifted a burden from her, or at the very least, made it lighter. She didn't have to carry it alone anymore.

She still couldn't sleep. Instead, she spent the night worrying the wraith would come for her. She had thought herself so composed, back in her home, when she had planned to travel to the mountains alone. *I wonder if I would have made it. Would I have turned tail and run again? Is that why the Fates brought Mendleson into my life?*

The thought only gave her another topic to keep her awake. His plan sounded good, but how would it really work out? Was there a way to change her fate? Was there a way to change his?

But what really bothered her was that she couldn't keep the picture of his face out of her mind. The way he looked at her, concern without reverence or fear. He cared about her, and she knew he thought it was an opportunity to correct for not saving his wife. Henrietta didn't care why, though. For the first time since her Gran passed away, someone cared, and it wasn't because of what she could do.

Henrietta was surprised at how long the morning took to come. She had thought it late when she tried leaving him, and with all that happened, she imagined the morning sun couldn't have been more than an hour or two away.

When it did come, she still hadn't slept, and felt so weary that she didn't want to get out of bed.

But she forced herself out anyway. She dressed in her other change of clothes and stepped out of her room. She smelled eggs and biscuits cooking, and followed her nose to find Gretta in the kitchen, humming.

"Have a seat," Gretta said, pointing to the table.

Henrietta took a seat, and moments later, Gretta put a plate and a fork in front of her. Henrietta loaded her fork with eggs and stuck them in her mouth. She felt them slide down her throat to warm her up.

"You look like you didn't sleep," Gretta said while sitting down across from her with her own plate.

"I didn't."

"Any particular reason?"

"First, I worried the wraith would show up here, but later, I started thinking about Mendleson."

"He cares for you."

"Does he? It seems that way, even to me. But I wonder if he's just helping me because of his wife." Henrietta took a bite of her biscuit. Gretta had buttered it for her already.

"He's married?"

Henrietta shook her head while she tried to swallow the biscuit. "No," she said once the biscuit was down. "Not anymore. His wife died in a fire a few years ago, along with their son. I've heard that he blames himself for not being there to save her."

"Where was he?"

"He was a fisherman. I think he was out on the water fishing."

Gretta looked thoughtful. The two of them ate in silence for a bit.

"So tell me about the festival," Gretta said, breaking the silence. "Why were you there? I've never known you to attend those things."

"I don't, usually. But I had a vision of myself going to the festival, so I went."

"What happened there?"

"Some women wanted me to see for them right then and there, but I couldn't see anything. I managed to escape and found myself next to Mendleson. We struck up a conversation, and then he asked me if there was any way he might have saved his wife."

"That's why you think he's helping you."

Henrietta nodded. "I moved to leave. He reached out and grabbed my hand, and I had the vision. I've tried everything I could think of to get him to leave, but he's so stubborn."

Gretta chuckled. "Henrietta, you had a vision of yourself going to the festival. You were supposed to meet Mendleson. You were supposed to have that vision. Why are you so certain your vision means doom?"

"The wraiths attack him, and when they come away, he's motionless on the ground. What else could it mean?"

"Henrietta, you've been alone your whole life."

Anger welled up within Henrietta. *Why would Gretta say that?* "What's that supposed to mean?"

"Do you know what love is?"

"It's what happens when two people like each other so much they can't bear to be apart."

Gretta laughed. "Love, Henrietta, is when a man drags a woman halfway across town to get help for her while he nearly bleeds his own life onto the street."

No. "But we hardly know each other."

"And what makes you think knowledge is a requirement for love?"

How can this be? I don't believe it. "If love is involved here, it's the love of his wife, not of me."

"It may have started that way, but I can only tell you what I saw. I saw a man who had more concern for you than for himself. He may not even know it yet. Most men are too thick-headed to understand what's happening."

"But..."

"Don't argue with me just for the sake of arguing. I'm an old woman, Henrietta, and I've seen the many relationships people have when their loved ones are dying. Listen to your heart, not your Sight. Try to understand what it's saying to you."

Henrietta finished the last of her breakfast. *Could she be right? What does it matter if she is? There's not enough time. I can't let him die for me.*

She stood up. Her legs felt stronger from the food, but still weary. "Thank you for the breakfast, Gretta."

"Where are you going?"

"I'm going to wake Mendleson. We should be on our way."

Gretta came around the table and gave Henrietta a hug. "I don't think so," she said. "Mendleson won't wake for hours, not after the draught I gave him finally took hold. And you need sleep, too."

Henrietta yawned. She did need sleep. "What about my things? Are they still at the inn? I should go get them."

"I'll have Brode retrieve them."

Gretta couldn't be right. *It's only been three days. Love doesn't happen that fast, does it? And what does it matter? I don't love him.*

Then she thought about the kiss in her vision that had seemed so real. *Maybe there's something to what Gretta says. But how do I listen to my heart?*

‡

Mendleson found Henrietta sitting at the end of his bed when he woke. He had no idea how long she'd been there, but it felt good to see her. He remembered a conversation taking place at some point. He had a vague memory of convincing her to let him protect her, but he couldn't quite figure out if it had been a dream or not.

Seeing her sitting there watching him indicated that maybe it had been real, after all.

"How are you feeling?" she asked.

Mendleson hadn't even noticed, but after her question, his aches impinged upon him.

"I've felt better. That wraith nearly got the better of me, didn't it." It certainly felt like it. If he didn't remember the thing going up in flames, he wouldn't have been surprised if it had won their battle.

"From what Gretta tells me, you're lucky to be alive."

"It's not luck," he said, and chuckled a little before the pain of it stopped him.

"What do you mean by that?"

"It's fate, isn't it? I can't die until your vision says I do."

Henrietta shook her head. "It doesn't work that way."

"It is dead, isn't it?" he asked.

"I don't know. It won't matter. Like I said last night, there are others that will come for me."

Mendleson sat up, despite the pain, and swung his legs out of the bed. They were bare. He silently thanked Gretta for not removing his underclothes. "I guess I'm not going far without my clothes." He looked at her. "Don't let that give you any ideas. I'd follow you without them."

She laughed, which brought his spirits up. He could not remember hearing her laugh before. "I'm sure you would. I've done everything I could to get rid of you."

"You haven't tried to kill me yet."

Her smile fell. "I'm trying to prevent your death, Mendleson. Not hasten it."

Mendleson looked down at his feet and flexed his toes. They were about the only part of him not bandaged. "I'm trying to do the same for you."

"Why? Because of your wife?"

"Partly," he said. "but I'm not sure anymore. I've saved you twice already. Why can't I just get on a horse and head home?"

"Why don't you?"

He looked back at her, saw her hair, her eyes that seemed so open, yet hid so much. *Why don't I?* She was at once, so strong, yet so vulnerable. "I don't know why," he said. "It just feels like I should stay with you."

"At risk of your life?"

"I made a promise to myself, Henrietta. I promised myself I wouldn't let you die."

Henrietta stood up. "You shouldn't have made that

promise, Mendleson. You should have left well enough alone."

"Maybe I should have. But it's too late now, isn't it? We're on this course, and we have to sail it."

Henrietta sighed, then walked to the door. She opened it and made as if to step out, then turned to face him.

"You know what Gretta said?"

Mendleson shook his head.

"She told me she thought you were in love with me."

"How is that possible?" he asked. "We've known each other three days." *It's not possible is it? Could I love her? No.*

"That's what I told her, but she seemed certain."

They stared at each other, he sitting on his bed, covered in bandages, her standing at the door, beautiful as ever.

"It doesn't matter, does it? Even if I was in love with you, you can't say the same thing about me, seeing as how you're always trying to get rid of me."

Mendleson watched her for a reaction, but she held her face still. "Of course not," she said. "You're too bull-headed for me. You should get ready to go. We have a long ride."

She turned and walked out the door, shutting it behind her with a loud bang.

"Wait! Where are my clothes?"

She didn't come back to answer him.

‡

Henrietta did not know how he had just made her so angry. *I'm only trying to protect you, you oaf. He's right anyway. How could it be love after three days of running and sleeping. I hardly know anything about you, either.*

She let herself fume in silence until she ran into Gretta. "Do you want to see if that fool is ready to go? I don't think we should stay another night."

"What's wrong, Henrietta?"

"Nothing." Apparently, she hadn't quite controlled her anger yet. "If we're going to do this, I think we need to get moving, and he's sitting around in there without any clothes on."

"You didn't tell him where they were?"

"I'd like you to examine him first. I don't want him dying on me."

"Oh, he's fine, as long as he doesn't exert himself too much for a few days."

"A few days?" *What if we're attacked again?*

"He should be good to ride. Just don't make him carry you to any more healers. I'll let him know where his clothes are. Brode has the horses out back."

"Thank you," Henrietta said.

Gretta left, and Henrietta made her way to the back of the house where Gretta had a stable.

Henrietta found Gretta's husband in the stable grooming horses, only they weren't the horses from the coach. The coach was missing, too. "Where is the coach?"

Brode made Mendleson look small. Henrietta could imagine he would appear to be a giant in the right lighting. Which made it all the more amusing when she talked with him. "I haven't seen you in a while, Brode."

"I saw you," he said, and rushed over to envelope her in a hug. His voice sounded like a child's. "You're lucky your friend brought you here, I think."

"What happened to our horses?"

"Gretta had me sell them, and the coach, too. She said where you were going, you might be better off with more speed, so we bought these."

Henrietta didn't have any eye for horses. They all pretty much looked the same to her, but she nodded anyway. "She's probably right." *Though I'm not in any hurry to hasten my death.*

Brode dug into his coat pocket and pulled out a purse that jingled. "This is yours, too. Leftovers from selling everything."

She took it and found it was heavy. It would probably be more useful than the coach.

Besides, this way, you won't have to sit next to him and talk for the whole trip. She couldn't decide whether that was really a benefit.

Mendleson stepped outside, a bit gingerly. Gretta followed him, carrying a pair of packs. Henrietta found herself wondering if leaving right now was a good idea. Perhaps they could wait another night.

"Are you sure you can do this?" she asked as Mendleson and Gretta entered the stable.

"Gretta assures me they're just flesh wounds, and that now they've scabbed over, I'll be fine as long as I don't exert myself too much. I've had worse injuries."

He looked around, then out through the stable door where dusk was just beginning to arrive. "We travel at night?" he asked.

"At least tonight," she said, feeling defensive.

"It's probably a good plan. At least we'll be awake when they attack us."

Gretta handed the packs to Brode, who draped them across the horses. "There are a few packages of herbs in your pack," she said to Henrietta. "If any of his wounds break open, pack the herbs in the wound and dress it again."

Henrietta nodded.

"He should be mostly better in a few days. Today and tomorrow will be the time to take the most care."

"Thank you, Gretta, for everything."

"I appreciate the thanks, but there is no need. You helped me long ago," she said, looking at Brode who was helping Mendleson into his saddle. "I am only returning the favor."

Henrietta leaned in and hugged Gretta. "You deserve my thanks anyway," she said. *Even if you're wrong about love.*

Henrietta mounted her horse without too much trouble.

She looked at Mendleson, wondered if she should say anything, then decided against it. Putting her heals into the horse, she directed it out into the early evening. She didn't wait to see if Mendleson followed.

She took a deep breath, inhaling the smells of salt air, knowing it would be the last time she smelled the sea.

Mendleson rode up next to her. "I'll miss that smell," he said.

She surprised herself. For the moment, she felt content. She was on her fated path with her fated company. It felt right.

Until she remembered where it lead, and her contentedness fell apart to shatter on the road.

EIGHT

Mendleson thought it fortunate that they were taking the trip in the middle of summer. They could travel light without the need for tents and heavy blankets, and the sky stayed clear, allowing the stars and the moon to light their way.

They followed the road out of town, still continuing south along the coast. He knew they would have to turn east at some point, as he was vaguely aware that Arabeth lay in that direction.

But he'd never been so far from home. Riding along the coast, it didn't look much different from his home. The moon reflected off the sea whenever it wasn't blocked by dunes or bluffs or the trees that grew on them.

The trees were the biggest difference. There were so many more of them dotting the hillsides. He didn't think there was room for farmland in any direction for miles.

On occasion, they passed a solitary home, the windows dark while its occupants slept.

Most of the time, when not keeping an eye out for wraiths, he watched Henrietta's back. He wondered what she was thinking, and he pondered the possible reasons she had grown so angry with him.

She couldn't possibly have feelings for him. Not after three days. She kept trying to get rid of him. She'd even tried to leave while he slept.

Even if she did feel something for him, his memory of Mirrielle would come between them, wouldn't it? But when he thought about it, he realized he hadn't dreamed of Mirrielle since meeting Henrietta, and he only thought of Mirrielle when Henrietta brought it up.

Are you telling me something Mirrielle? I'm not ready.

"Mendleson."

"What?" He looked up and found that they had come to a road that lead east, and Henrietta had turned down it while he'd been... *What was I doing exactly?*

He brought his horse around to follow her, and waved a mental goodbye to the sea.

"I hope Paulus came looking for me and took care of my animals," he said.

"What?"

"My animals. My horse, the sheep. I hope someone found them and took care of them. I feel like I won't see them again."

"You'll see them again."

"Will I? Will I even go back there again?" He thought about Paulus. Hugh. "Damn."

"What?"

"They're probably all looking for us."

"They'll look for you. Me, they'll assume I got on the coach."

In the starlight, all he could see of her was her silhouette.

"Why are you so melancholy of a sudden?" she asked.

He looked back over his shoulder, and the sea had disappeared. "I've always lived near the sea, even as a boy. It's a part of me, and I'm leaving it behind."

She didn't say anything for a moment, and Mendleson began to think she wouldn't say anything at all. The only sound was the thud of the horses hooves on the packed dirt road.

She surprised him when she spoke again. "When I left my home, I think I felt much the same as you. I feared I would never return. I feared I would miss the trees and the stone.

"And, for a while, I did miss them. But I found new things to see and love. The sound of the waves as they break upon shore, the view of the sea, the sound of the wind as it roars off the water.

"You will find new things, too, if you choose not to return. Do not mourn your past. There is always a future."

Mendleson liked listening to her, even if the last bit sounded like rote Seer wisdom. Her voice had a soothing quality to it, when she chose to use it.

"Do you believe that?" he asked.

"Believe what?"

"That there is always a future." As soon as he finished, he wished he could have the words back. He knew the answer she would give, and he felt like fish guts for making her think it.

Before she could respond, he said, "I'm sorry. I shouldn't have asked that."

"No, it's all right," she said. "You weren't asking about me."

"No, I wasn't." he said.

"Do you want to talk about it?"

He thought back to the memory, the days after, the years since. They still hurt, even though he now felt like he had a purpose for the first time since the moment he'd discovered Mirrielle and Josua dead at the center of his burnt out house.

"Not right now," he said, and let his horse drop back behind hers. He hadn't thought about them deeply for days, but the night-time ride gave him ample time to think.

‡

Henrietta called a halt to their ride as they entered a small village just after dawn. Children were already up and playing in the gaps between the houses. Men readied themselves for the fields and other professions.

It had a small inn, and she found herself knocking on the door while Mendleson tied up their horses. She looked back at him while she waited for the proprietor to open the door. He hadn't said a word since she asked if he wanted to talk about his future. She suspected, however, it wasn't his future he mulled over, but his past.

That question had somehow caused him to revert to the man he'd been for the four years prior to the festival.

The door opened, and she found herself confronted by a man that appeared to be three times her age. His head grew only a white fringe of hair around its crown, and his nose hooked down so that it nearly obscured his upper lip. His bones looked ready to split his skin if he sat or moved the wrong way.

"What's this, you bothering us so early with your bangin'?" he asked.

"I'm sorry," she said, trying to look contrite. She had thought he would be up and about with his guests already. "My..." she looked at Mendleson, "husband and I need a room for the day."

"For the day? What sort of folk are you that you need a room for the day?"

"Just travelers. Please sir, we've been riding all night, and just need a safe place to sleep."

A hand reached around the door and pulled it open wider, revealing a stout woman that stood more than a foot shorter than the man. Her girth more than made up for the difference.

"Give the dears a room old man," she said. "They look exhausted. Have your husband..." Henrietta heard a cough behind her, but didn't turn around, "...take the horses around back to the stable."

"Thad, go take care of those horses," the woman said. She reached out her hand to Henrietta. "Come in, dear. He's just ornery in the morning."

Henrietta took her hand. As the woman pulled her into the inn, Henrietta looked over her shoulder and saw Mendleson leading the horses away. *I hope he has the good sense to play along.*

The woman led her into a dining area that looked to take up most of the first floor of the inn. It was empty of patrons.

"Do you not have many guests?" Henrietta asked.

"Some days, we have several, other days, none. Last night was one of the latter. Those days makes Thad testy. Here, sit a moment."

She pulled out a chair for Henrietta, and Henrietta sat in it, despite not having much desire to sit. She hadn't ridden a horse so far in years, and she felt sore all over, but mostly in the parts she was sitting on.

"Would you dears need to eat something before I show you a room?" the woman asked.

"What do you have?"

"I could heat up bread and broth right quick. We weren't much prepared for guests this morning."

Henrietta sighed. She'd much prefer eggs or salted pork. "That'll be fine," she said.

Mendleson came into the room from the back carrying their packs. He set the packs down next to the table, pulled a chair out, and sat down much like Henrietta imagined Thad would sit. "Why are we sitting? I just want to lay down and sleep."

"She's making us something to eat."

"A slab of roast?" he asked.

Her mouth watered. "Bread and broth."

"That'll do," he said, crossed his arms on the table and laid his head on them. Henrietta had an urge to reach out and run her fingers through his hair, but she kept her hand to herself.

They waited that way until the woman came out with a tray. On it rested two steaming bowls and a plate with bread. Mendleson lifted his head up.

She set the tray on the table, placed a bowl in front of each of them, and set the bread plate in the middle.

"Let me know when you dears are ready for your room, and I'll take ya up."

"Thank you."

The woman walked away and left them alone.

"So," Mendleson said in a low voice, "why did you tell them I was your husband?"

"I thought it would forestall strange questions."

"You could just as easily have said I was your guardian, like we did last time."

"I didn't want to let them know what I am, and I wanted us in the same room."

"Why?"

"In these small towns, Seers can be overwhelmed with requests for visions, if they're not run out of town. You never know what will happen."

"No," he said. "Why did you want us in the same room?"

"To save money," she said, not wanting to examine her motives. She didn't want to admit to not knowing why she did it. She didn't want to admit to the possibility that she did.

"We have plenty of money," he said.

"Just eat. We'll discuss it in the room."

He stared at her. She stared back, and for a moment, she thought she could see into his mind, and into his past. Then he broke eye contact, picked up his spoon and scooped broth into his mouth.

They finished their meal in silence. When they were done, the woman appeared out of nowhere, as if she had been watching them.

"Are you ready for your room?" she asked.

"Please," Henrietta said, and stood.

Mendleson stood, too, then picked up their packs.

They followed the woman up a stairwell near the back of the inn and then down a hallway until she reached the end. She opened a door on the right, then stood there while they entered the room. It looked nice for a room in a village this small. Henrietta suspected it was their best room.

It had a bed, a wash basin, and a rocking chair. A poorly executed painting of the Fates hung above the bed. Henrietta looked back at the woman. *Does she know?* But the woman wasn't looking at her. She was instead engaged in getting payment from Mendleson.

"Ma'am, would you mind waking us just before dusk," Henrietta asked.

The woman closed her fleshy fist around the coin Mendleson had just placed in her palm and looked up. "Of course," she said. "Just before dusk. Will you want something to eat before you leave?"

Henrietta looked to Mendleson, who was looking at her. She couldn't read his expression. "That would be nice," she said. It would certainly be better than eating on the road.

"I'll see to it, then," the woman said. "Have a good rest." She turned and walked down the hall.

Mendleson closed the door. She saw him eye the bed, then the window. The window had curtains, but they weren't at all thick. She watched him go to the bed and pull a blanket off.

"What are you doing?" she asked.

He took the blanket to the window. "I'm going to cover the window." He hung the blanket up on the curtain rod, and the room grew much darker.

He went back to the bed, took hold of the other blanket and pulled it off.

"What are you doing now?"

In the darkness, he looked puzzled. "I'm going to lay this out under me so that I don't have to sleep directly on the floor."

Henrietta felt her heart beat a little faster. "You don't have to sleep on the floor. There's room for both of us on the bed."

She could see his head turn as he looked between her and the bed.

"Are you sure?"

She imagined laying next to him, feeling his body against hers. *What will it feel like to touch him? To feel his warmth so close?* It was possible he would be her last chance to find out what a man felt like so close.

"I'm sure," she said. *Really?* But she wanted it. She wanted to know.

He put the blanket back, then went around to the other side of the bed, putting it in between them.

He unlaced his shirt, and she found herself watching him. As the shirt came away, it exposed the bandages he wore underneath. A stray sunbeam caught one of them, and she thought she saw red where blood had soaked through.

Damn. She had forgotten about his wounds. "I should not have let you carry those bags," she said. "Sit down."

"What?"

"I think you ripped open one of the wounds. Come over here and sit on the bed next to the lamp, and I'll tend to it."

She went to the nightstand and lit the lamp, bringing the light up enough to see. He came around and sat down. Up close, she saw that two of the bandages were red with his blood.

She searched through her pack until she found the herb packages Gretta had stowed inside. She took out two of them, and brought them to the bed. Gretta had thought to wrap the packages in additional bandages, for which Henrietta silently thanked her.

Looking at the wounds, she decided the worst one was the one on his side. She reached around him to get at where the bandage had been tied off, which brought her face close to his chest. She could smell him, and far from being unpleasant, it made her want to lay her head on his chest.

She almost did before she remembered what she was doing and untied the bandage. She had to reach around him more than once to unwrap it, and every time, it brought her in close to him.

When the bandage was completely free, she looked down and saw the damage the wraith had done to him, and she hissed. It was far worse than she had imagined. There were cuts all over his torso. "How did you even manage to ride today?" she whispered.

"I didn't ride on my belly," he said.

She found the wound that was bleeding the most. It was a six inch gash on his side, just below his ribs.

She went to the washbasin, which she found full of water. A couple cloths were next to it. Henrietta silently thanked the woman for seeing to their needs. She picked up one of the cloths, dipped it in the water, then went back and knelt down in front of Mendleson.

She wiped the blood away from the wound and saw that it had only pulled open enough to bleed a bit and make a mess. Mendleson didn't move under her ministrations.

"Doesn't this hurt?" she asked.

"Of course it does," he said.

"Then why don't you move?"

"If I moved, everything else would hurt."

Henrietta laughed, and she had to pull her hand away from him until she could stop.

"Why are you laughing?" he asked.

"I don't know," she said. "You're just so contradictory."

"I don't understand."

She looked up into his eyes, and they were watching her. "You sit here, not moving, in order to avoid additional pain. Yet you insist on coming with me wherever I go, knowing that my vision says your path will end in your death."

His eyes kept watching hers, but he didn't open his mouth to say anything. She wondered what he was thinking. She wondered if, perhaps, he was thinking about his wife.

"I'm sorry," she said, looking away. "Maybe it isn't that funny."

She reached over and grabbed a packet of herbs. She pinched some out, and then began packing them into his wound. He did flinch, then. After she finished packing the wound, she wrapped the bandage around him again.

His closeness seemed different this time. More comforting, less exciting.

"No," he said. "You don't have to be sorry."

"But..." she tried to protest.

He put his fingers to her mouth to stop her. "We're both tired. And you are right. It is a contradiction, but it's not one I'm sure I can explain."

He stood up, walked around to the other side of the bed, then climbed on it, and lay on his back.

Henrietta took the bloodied cloth to the washbasin where she set it to the side. She picked up the other cloth, dipped it in the water, and wiped her face.

The washbasin had a mirror above it that let her see Mendleson lying in bed while she cleaned up. With his wounds and the long horse-ride, she realized she'd have to wait before she could discover what it meant to be a woman. *I wonder if Gretta was laughing when she told me he had to avoid anything strenuous. Did she know what I might do?*

She searched through their packs until she found a nightgown. She looked at Mendleson and saw he had his eyes closed. She stripped off her clothes as quickly as she could and slipped into the gown.

She climbed into bed, blew out the lamp, then lay her head down. After a moment, when Mendleson hadn't moved, she rolled to face him, and she moved in close enough that she could breathe in his scent while she slept.

NINE

Over the next three nights, Mendleson could feel he was getting better. The minor cuts and scrapes had ceased to pain him. Only the major ones, the large tear on his side, and two others on his back, caused him any discomfort.

Henrietta had to apply the herbs to at least one of the three each morning after they'd come to a halt. Despite the pain it caused him, he found he didn't mind her ministrations. He didn't know if she was aware of what she was doing to him, but each day, he found it harder and harder to remain stoic while she attended to his wounds, especially during the moments when she was unwrapping the bandages.

One of the days, they'd found another inn to sleep at, but it had been full of rats and had an underlying musty smell, even in the heat of the summer. He hadn't slept well at all. When he mentioned to Henrietta that he wished they'd slept outdoors, she had agreed.

The other two days, they'd had to find spots deep in the forest and away from the road to sleep the day away. He had worried about bandits, but she told him not to worry. His worry, it had turned out, had been for naught. No one came and stole their things or accosted them while they slept.

So when they reached the border city of Berelost a couple hours before sunrise, he had hope that they could find an inn that would allow him to get a good day's sleep.

They emerged from the forest into a large clearing that surrounded the city. It was dotted with darkened homes. In the distance, lamplight lit the thirty foot tall city walls. They were a relic of the distant past when wars raged across the lands and each city had to look to its own protection.

Mendleson had never seen the city before. "I would have thought they would have abandoned the walls long ago," he said to Henrietta.

"The memories in Berelost are long, and they do not look much to the future. The wars were hard on them."

"You know this place well?" he asked.

"I spent a year here, before I moved to Porthead."

"Why did you leave?"

"They asked me to," she said.

Mendleson thought about asking her to elaborate, but decided against it. She didn't sound like she wanted to talk about it.

As they approached the walls, they found the immense gate shut.

They sat atop their horses and waited at the gate for several minutes, but the guards were either asleep, or ignoring them in the hope they would go away.

"Do you want to see if they will let us in?"

Henrietta pulled at the reins of her horse. "No, there are only a couple hours at most before they open the gate. No need to bother them."

Mendleson followed her, while wondering at her quick dismissal of his idea. He couldn't imagine that asking would cause that much trouble.

Henrietta found a place away from the wall that was sheltered by a hedge. It had a nearby fence where they could tie up the horses.

Mendleson couldn't contain his curiosity. "Why didn't you want to ask them to let us in?" he asked while they tied their horses to separate fence posts.

"First, we'd have to tell them who we are, and then somehow convince them our mission was urgent."

"It is urgent," Mendleson said. "I need to find a bed."

Henrietta finished tying her horse and went to sit up against the hedge. Moments later, Mendleson finished with his horse, and he walked over and sat next to her.

"Do you need a bed so much that you're willing to risk getting tossed from that bed?" she asked.

"What are you talking about?" Mendleson ran his fingers through the grass.

MARK FASSETT

"Remember how I told you that they asked me to leave? They warned me to never come back."

Mendleson looked up. He could see the outline of her head against the glow created by the lamps along the walls. She was looking at those walls. "What did they say would happen?"

"They accused me of inciting lawlessness."

Mendleson laughed. "You?"

"As I said, they prefer to look to the past. Their current status as just another city eats at their hearts."

"Let me guess. You told someone important of their future, and they didn't like it."

Henrietta laughed for the first time since they'd left Gretta's. Her laugh had a musical quality to it that warmed him and, for a moment, reminded him of better times. "Hardly," she said. "I told an unscrupulous street vendor that I saw him in prison in the not too distant future. I had no idea what would land him there. I assumed it was his various tricks that would find him a free bed. Instead, he decided to try to kill the magistrate."

"He didn't succeed?"

"No," she said without the laughter, "which is how he only ended up in prison, and I ended up leaving with the gate shut behind me."

Mendleson looked out over the darkened landscape and contemplated what happened to her. After minutes of silence, he said, "You don't think your vision for his future prompted him to fulfill that destiny, do you?"

"Are you asking if I think I should have withheld that particular future from him?"

"Do you?"

"The Fates are fickle and hard to decipher, even in the most obvious situations. If I had withheld that future from him, would I have caused him to do something else that landed him in prison? By telling him, I gave him the opportunity to change his ways and perhaps avoid prison. He made a different choice."

"But if you hadn't told him," Mendleson said, "you might not have had to leave Berelost. You might not have come to Porthead."

"But the Fates might have found another way to drive me toward my destiny. The vision I've had of my death since I was six has not changed in all these years—not until I met you. Even then, all I managed to do in my effort to avoid my fate is put you in the middle of it with me. My fate hasn't changed, no matter what I've done.

"Are my visions given to me in order that I may try to change them? Or are they given to me so that I may tell the person involved so that they can try to change things? I can't make that decision Mendleson. It's not my decision to make."

Mendleson looked at her again and saw she was staring straight ahead. He could see the slight crook of her nose as a silhouette. He found himself watching it, hoping she would turn it in his direction, hoping she would look at him. *You confound me, Henrietta. You do everything you can to push me away, yet I'm drawn to try to save you as if you were family.*

He didn't even want to think about what that meant for his memory of his wife and son. He'd hardly thought of them in days. Upon realizing it, he felt his spirits sink, but they did not sink as far as he thought they should. Some other spirit buoyed them against the weight of his wife and his son.

For a moment, he felt like reaching out and hugging Henrietta to him. He needed her contact, but he refrained. *It won't do to get involved with her in that way, Mendleson. If she's right, you'll be dead in a few weeks or less.*

But what if she's seeing it wrong? What if she's misinterpreting it like she did with the street merchant?

Mendleson couldn't come to any conclusions while they sat next to each other in silence. After an hour or so, the sky grew lighter, and in the distance, he saw the gates to the city open.

"This will be my first time in a city," Mendleson said as he untied his horse.

"Don't worry about it. We'll only be here a day."

‡

Henrietta told herself, over and over as they entered the city, that she would make it through without any trouble. She felt confident they would make it through. In order for her vision to come to pass, they would have to. It was the "without any trouble" part that she worried about.

She'd lived within the stone walls, thicker than the length of a horse, for a year. She had to work to hold back those memories as she passed through the gate in the early morning light.

Berelost lived in its memories of previous glories. It had stood for centuries, dividing the kingdoms on either side, standing apart from them, until the day those two kingdoms became one. That new, unified kingdom spent all its might for three years on Berelost, and finally cracked it. Even now, a lifetime later, they remembered what they had been.

She led Mendleson through the still shadowed streets. She looked back over her shoulder and saw that his mouth hung open and his eyes constantly moved from one sight to another. She caught herself smiling and turned away, hoping he didn't see it.

She did look around herself. The two and three story buildings loomed over the street, closer than she remembered. She knew people lived in them, above their shops, and that they weren't really trying to crush her, but she couldn't rid herself of the feeling that the city knew who she was and it didn't want her there. Even after three years, her memories of this place clouded her perception of it.

She quit looking around and concentrated on her path through the maze of streets. The main road they had entered on did not drive straight through to the heart of the city. It meandered about, visiting many of the burroughs, until it finally reached the river that separated the eastern half of the city from its western half, and gave Berelost its reason for being.

Buildings could not be built out into the road at ground level. The law required that builders had to leave enough room for carriages to pass each other at any point. Above the ground floor, the builders were allowed to build as they pleased. As a result, the buildings hung out over the road, almost like their purpose was to block out the sky.

Henrietta looked up through a gap above her and saw that the morning was not dawning blue and bright, but cloudy and gray.

"Mendleson," she said.

He stopped his gawking and pulled up next to her. "I don't like this place," he said. "It makes me feel like I'm in a barrel."

"You might have to get used to it," she said.

"Why?"

"The sky, it has clouded over. There's a storm coming, I think."

"A vision?" he asked.

She shook her head. "No vision, just experience. They sometimes get late summer storms here that last for days. The year I lived here, rain fell and the wind blew for nearly a week. I couldn't go outside for fear of losing my footing."

"What should we do then? We can't stop moving, can we?"

"I don't know. We might not have a choice."

She watched Mendleson rock his head back and yawn. "Should we just push through?"

"You'll fall asleep on your horse. No, we need to rest." She patted her pack. It was almost empty. "We need to purchase more supplies, too."

She kept them moving, passing denizens of the city as they stepped outside their doors to head off to work, or to open their shops. The streets grew more and more choked with people as they drew close to the river.

When they reached the mall along the riverfront, it was already crowded, making it difficult to maneuver their horses with any speed. Over the top of the crowd, she could see the three bridges that spanned the murky channel of water. North of them, the docks were already busy with people readying their boats for trading voyages up and down the river.

She looked back and caught Mendleson looking that way, an expression of longing on his face.

"Do you miss it?" she asked him. She had to raise her voice to be heard over the noise of the mall.

He turned to look at her. "What?"

"Do you miss your boat, miss going out on the water?"

He stared at her for a moment, then glanced back over his shoulder at the docks. "No," he said, finally, shaking his head. "It was another life."

To Henrietta, he sounded like he was trying to convince himself.

Then he changed the subject on her. "Where are we going?"

She wanted to ask what he meant about it being another life, but decided to let it lie until later. "An inn on the other side of the river. I have a friend there." *I think.*

"Then lead on," he said, a hint of anger in his voice.

She couldn't figure out what she'd done to upset him, but decided the mall was not the place to ask. It probably didn't help matters that they were both tired. She wasn't meant for traveling at night and sleeping during the day. She almost hoped they'd have to stay in for a couple days due to the storm. But then, she didn't want to risk having the wraith appear. She didn't want to risk having Mendleson foolishly try to save her again.

As she rode through the crowd and brought them across the middle bridge, a solid stone monstrosity wide enough for an army to cross, her thoughts turned to ways she could prevent Mendleson from helping her. Not one of the ways she could imagine had a real possibility of working.

Trying to leave while he slept seemed possible, but she couldn't bring herself to do it. The only way it could succeed is if she left him without his horse and without the money to purchase another. The problem was that it would leave him stranded, far from his home, with possibly no way to return.

It didn't help, either, that she liked having him around. Except for the times when his mood grew sour after she brushed up against his previous life, either intentionally or on accident, he was easy company. He didn't talk too much, didn't press her for visions about his future. Of course, she'd already told him of his future.

She looked back at him. He had his head down, letting his horse follow hers. He'd stopped looking around and appeared to have sunk inward. She wanted to reach back somehow and put her arm around him, help him deal with his past. *If only I knew how.*

A man shouted at her. "Watch where you're going!"

She turned around to find that she'd almost ridden her horse into a portly man dressed in a black suit, the jacket of which strained against the man's middle. Streaks of gray ran through his dark hair, and he wore a mustache, the ends of which hung down below his chin.

She recognized him and her heart skipped a beat. He hadn't changed much in the three years she'd been absent. *Fates! Why do I have to run into the Magistrate?* "I'm sorry," she said, turning her head away slightly, as if ashamed. She hoped it would be enough. She hoped three years was enough.

His eyes searched her. *Please don't recognize me.* She hoped the dirt of the road, the unwashed nature of her clothes, the undone state of her hair, would be enough to make her unrecognizable. She felt Mendleson come up beside her.

"Do I know you?" the magistrate asked.

"No," she said, trying to act meek.

Mendleson leaned out in front of her. "Excuse my wife, sir. We are just passing through, and she is new to riding."

The Magistrate's gaze drifted to Mendleson as Mendleson spoke, but as soon as Mendleson finished, it flicked back to Henrietta. "Well," he said, his eyes not leaving her, "perhaps you should lead her through the city, then."

"Yes, yes," Mendleson said. "I shall do that." He took the reins of her horse from her, and started to lead her on. "Let's go, Mathilda."

She kept one eye on the Magistrate for as long as she was able, while trying to hide her relief and surprise at Mendleson's quick thinking. The Magistrate turned and watched them go. He clearly recognized her, but couldn't place her face.

She waited until they were around a corner before she pulled her reins back from Mendleson's grasp.

"So who was that?" Mendleson asked.

"The Magistrate." She watched alarm grow in his face.

"Should we just leave the city?"

Henrietta thought it over, and realized this might be her chance. The wraith would come for her wherever she was. She could save Mendleson this way. *If only I'd thought of it while the Magistrate stood right next to me.* "We could leave, but by nightfall, we'd be exhausted. The horses need rest and feed. We still have to purchase supplies. I think we have to risk that he won't remember me."

"But he does remember you," Mendleson said. "It was clear from the way he couldn't stop looking at you."

"He remembers my face. He didn't connect it with who I am, or he wouldn't have allowed us to ride away."

"But what if he does figure it out? What if he has already and is looking for us? I think we should go, now."

"Mendleson, Berelost is a large city. Even if he makes the connection, he will have difficulty finding us before we leave."

Mendleson turned away from her for a moment. He had to go along with it.

When he turned back, he said, "Only for the morning. You're right, of course, we do need sleep, but I don't think we should stay any longer than we have to. This place feels dangerous to me."

That'll be long enough. "This way, then," she said, pulling her horse back into the lead. "We'll go to the inn, sleep until midday, then pick up supplies on our way out."

A gust of cold wind blew through the street, whipping her hair about her head. She looked up and saw the clouds above them had grown thicker and darker. *If only the storm will stay away.*

TEN

The inn that Henrietta led them to looked old and weather-worn to Mendleson's eye. Like the rest of the buildings in this strange city, it leaned out over the street, giving him the impression that it was near to toppling over on him.

When they climbed down from their horses, a dark-haired young boy, perhaps twelve, ran out from the inn and reached for the reins. "I'll take those," he said.

Mendleson looked to Henrietta, and saw her give the horse over to the boy. "You've grown, Perry."

"Ma'am?" the boy asked, his voice breaking as he spoke.

"You don't remember me? I suppose it has been a long time, then. Is your mother here?"

"In the kitchen," the boy said, clearly confused by Henrietta.

"Thank you," she said, pulling a coin from her purse and handing it to the boy, who smiled.

Mendleson handed the reins of his horse to the boy, and got a frown when he did not produce a coin, too.

"She has all my coins," he said.

The boy glanced at Henrietta, and when she nodded, his frown flattened, but did not entirely go away. The boy led the horses away, leaving the two of them standing at the doorway.

"You've been here before?" he asked.

"His mother was a friend."

"Was? Are you worried that she's not anymore?"

Henrietta's shoulders came up, and she raised her head and began to walk into the building. "There's no reason she shouldn't be a friend."

Mendleson reached out and tried to grab her arm, but she walked forward with a purpose, and his hand slid down to touch hers.

She stopped and gasped.

Mendleson knew what he'd done wrong before she told him, and he tried to let go, but she grasped his hand tight and wouldn't let him pull free. She turned to face him. Her eyes were open, the irises rolled back into her head far enough that he could not see them. They stood that way for only moments, though it seemed he could have planted next year's crops in the time it took her to come out of it.

Her eyes closed, and when they reopened, he could again see the dark of her eyes. She glanced down at his hand, which still held hers, but she made no immediate effort to pull away. He was glad of it. Her hand felt small and warm in his. Soft.

"What did you see?" he asked.

She blinked, then looked out to the street. Mendleson followed her gaze and found people were watching them. Not many, but enough.

She dropped his hand. "Nothing new," she said. She pushed open the thick wood door of the inn and stepped inside.

"Are you coming?" she asked, her back still to him.

Mendleson quickly stepped through the door, and she let it shut behind him.

Inside, he found the interior of the inn in much better shape than the outside. The wood tables were polished, clean, and in good repair. The floor was clear of debris, and the walls, where they were lined with wood, were varnished and free of the soot he'd become used to in the more run-down inns they had stayed in. It felt like a home. He wondered at the clash between the run-down exterior and the well cared for interior. Why would the owner not take care of the outside, too?

Henrietta strode through the main room, past the few patrons who had risen so early. Most of them looked well off, and certainly not the kind of patron he'd expected from the outside. It baffled him.

When Mendleson caught up to her, she had stopped just outside the kitchen door. The smell of morning cakes and sausage seeped through the door, giving Mendleson's stomach cause to rumble. "This place is so well cared for on the inside..." he said before being interrupted as the door swung open.

A woman, a head and a half shorter than Henrietta, stepped through the door carrying a tray with the cakes and sausages he had smelled piled onto it. She looked very much like the boy who had come to take their horses.

"Out of the way," she said, her voice powerful and commanding.

Mendleson stepped aside and let her pass. Henrietta had done the same, and the woman swept between them, leaving the two of them to look at each other. A fleeting emotion, irritation, or perhaps surprise, passed across Henrietta's face as the woman passed without so much as a greeting. Whatever emotion had overcome her control for the moment was buried before Mendleson could say for sure what it was.

Mendleson turned to watch the woman as she moved through the common room, setting food out in front of several of the early morning patrons. She had words with each of them, but didn't linger long with any particular patron.

After she emptied her tray, the woman returned. She kept her face free of emotion, but when she said, "Into the kitchen," he could hear the conflict within her.

Once the three of them were inside the kitchen, she set the tray on a free table top, and then went to Henrietta and gave her a hug. Then she stepped back and said, "How dare you come back here." Her voice seethed with anger and fear.

"I had to," Henrietta said.

"You had to do nothing of the sort. You know what will happen to you if they find you."

Henrietta nodded. "I know, but I truly have no choice. I'm going home, Tara."

Tara put a hand to her mouth, and then stepped forward and gave Henrietta another, much longer hug. "Surely not so soon," she said.

Henrietta patted the shorter woman on the back. "Weeks at most, if not days," she said. "It is the way of things."

Tara stepped away from the embrace. "But how can that be? You're still so young."

"I've known for a long time."

Tara turned to face Mendleson for the first time. She looked him up and down, seeming to appraise him like she would a cow, or perhaps a side of beef. "So who is this?" she asked once she finished.

"I'm Mendleson," he said, even though she hadn't directed the question at him. "I'm helping her."

Tara turned back to Henrietta. "Since when did you need help?" she asked.

Mendleson found Henrietta's eyes looking at him now, though her appraisal was different. He thought he saw sadness in it, and something else he could not quite make out. "I didn't ask for it," she said. A chill had crept into her voice that he hadn't heard for days.

There. She was still trying to push him away, still

trying to protect him from whatever fate she saw for him. *But I can't let her push me away. I can't let her die. I promised.*

Henrietta turned back to Tara. "But, he has been useful."

Useful! Anger boiled up in him, causing him to clench his fists. His fingernails bit into the palms of his hands. "I've saved your life more than once."

She stepped into him, and looked up, just a little. "How do you know, Mendleson? How do you know that your interference saved my life? Until you became involved, I knew my fate, and it was not at my front door, or in the hallway of that inn, or any other place on this journey."

"My interference? You came to me at the festival. I didn't set this course. Before that moment, I had little interest in you." Even as he said it, he found himself wondering how it had happened. He couldn't keep his curiosity contained. "Did you do something to me? Did you put some sort of spell on me?"

Her hand rose up and slapped him, almost before the last word had left his lips. "How dare you." Her voice raised only a little in her anger. "I am not a witch, Mendleson. You know that."

"Do I?" He thought back to that moment at the festival when they had touched. His life had changed in that moment. From that point, all he'd wanted to do was protect her. "I thought I wanted to protect you because I'd failed with Mirrielle, but now I'm not so sure. We touched and my life changed because of it."

"Keep your voice down," Henrietta said.

"Why? You keep trying to push me away. It's all you've done since that night, yet you tied a rope to me that even a typhoon couldn't break."

"Just how did I tie a rope to you? You've been free to leave me alone since that day at the festival. You're free to go even now. I don't need your help, Mendleson." She was staring right into his eyes as she said it.

He tried to probe their depths, but whatever warmth he'd thought he'd seen growing there was gone. He didn't even know what he'd done to bring about the change in her.

The thing that really surprised him was how his anger turned to ashes as she spoke. She seemed to truly mean what she said. She didn't want him. *Why am I here?*

The answer that had brought him to Berelost, that he was trying to save her, no longer felt like enough.

A silence stretched between them for long moments. Tara looked back and forth between them, but said nothing. The tension Mendleson felt between Henrietta and himself seemed to hold the brash woman back.

Henrietta reached into her pack and her hand emerged with the purse. She held it out to him.

"What's this?" Mendleson asked.

"For your trip home." Her hand shook.

"But..."

"Don't worry, Mendleson. I have means."

He reached out and took the purse from her, taking care not to brush her hand again. He reached in and pulled out a silver durin, turned away from Henrietta and handed it to Tara. "Could you find me a room? I need to rest."

As she put the coin into her pocket, Tara said, "Of course." Her eyes still flicked toward Henrietta, as if she were asking permission.

When Henrietta said nothing, Tara said, "Come, follow me," and then stepped out of the kitchen.

Mendleson turned to follow her, then looked back. "I'll be here until tomorrow, if you change your mind."

"Take care, Mendleson," she said.

Mendleson stepped out of the kitchen and let the door shut behind him. He'd thought closing the door might cut the rope that tied her to him, but he could still feel it pulling at him. He wanted to rush back in, tell her he wasn't leaving her, no matter what she said she wanted.

But as he followed Tara up the stairs at the back of the inn, he resolved that he would try to forget her. He hoped it would be easier than trying to forget his failure to save his family.

‡

Henrietta watched him walk out the door, the money purse in his hand, his pack slung from his shoulder, and felt a void envelope her. She felt a desire to reach out and stop him, pull him back to her, take back every word she'd said. She didn't want him to go. She wanted him near her.

But she steeled herself. She had to make him leave in order to protect him. She'd brought him into her fate somehow, and it was her responsibility to get him out of it. She couldn't let him die to save her when she knew there wasn't a chance his sacrifice would save her. The vision hadn't changed. The wraiths would still come for her, even as he lay dying at the top of that foggy plateau.

She wanted to touch him, one last time, to see if she had changed his fate. She'd hoped their hands would meet when he took the purse from her, but he had been careful not to touch her. *I should have reached out for him*, she thought, then chided herself for thinking it. *If I reached out, he wouldn't have left.* "Better to let him go and not know the answer," she said aloud in an attempt to convince herself that she had made the right choice.

It didn't work. She could almost feel the rope Mendleson described, stretching out through the closed door, pulling at her to go to him. But she stayed in the kitchen, out of sight of the patrons of the inn.

"Why are you crying, Ma'am?"

Henrietta looked around and found Perry standing there watching her. He'd snuck into the kitchen without making a sound.

"I'm not crying."

"But the tears," he said.

"Tears?" she asked, while moving a hand up to her face. "There aren't any..." She stopped when her hand discovered her cheek was wet.

She scrambled to come up with an excuse while she wiped the tears away. "Oh, I'm just so happy," she said, trying to smile. "I haven't seen your mother in such a long time." She hoped Perry would believe her.

Perry looked around, and then came back to her. "My mother's not here," he said.

"No, dear. She just stepped out to take my friend to his room." *My friend? When did that happen?*

"Do you need breakfast? I can help you find a table. Mother doesn't like customers in the kitchen."

Henrietta did smile, this time for real. She hoped it meant the end of her tears. "I'm not exactly a customer," she said. "I'm a friend, and I need to speak with your mother. I would like something to eat, if you have it. I've been on the road a long time."

Perry smiled and went to work, gathering up a plate and dishing up pork and bread. Henrietta watched him work, remembering back to when the boy had been mostly a nuisance, getting under his mother's feet. He'd grown up quite a bit in three years.

Tara entered the kitchen just as Perry handed Henrietta the plate. The smell of the food caused her stomach to rumble in anticipation. She hadn't eaten since the previous evening. She went to reach into her purse to get Perry another coin, only remembering at the last moment that she'd given it all to Mendleson. "I'm sorry, Perry. I seem to have misplaced my purse. I'll have to get you another coin a little later."

"No you didn't," he said. "I saw you give it to that man."

"So I did," she said, surprised he'd seen that. He'd stabled their horses pretty quickly. "I promise I'll get you another coin before I leave."

Tara took Perry by the shoulders and pushed him out into the common room. "Go clean those tables," she said.

Perry turned a bit to look at Henrietta, and smiled at her before leaving the kitchen completely.

"It seems he likes you," Tara said when the door had swung shut.

"What? I hadn't even thought of that," she laughed. "He's grown so big."

"It's been three years," Tara said. "Boys grow like weeds."

"Yet it seems you've managed to tame him."

Tara laughed. "Mostly. He still has his days where I'm lucky to get him to feed the horses without a struggle. Come, I'll get you something to wash down that pork and we can talk."

Henrietta took a seat at a small table in the back of the kitchen that Tara reserved for eating quick lunches out of sight of her customers. "But it's still near breakfast. Don't you need to watch the room?"

"Perry's out there. He'll let me know if someone needs help, and I'm not letting you out of this kitchen without knowing the real story behind this man you brought with you. Water, or wine?"

Henrietta sat her plate on the table and took one of the chairs. There were only ever two chairs. "Wine, I think. I need to calm myself so I can sleep."

Tara stepped away for a moment, which gave Henrietta time to sample the food on her plate. The bread was warm and soft, the pork, not too salty. She wished for a moment that Tara would take her time so that she could eat more of it before having to talk about Mendleson.

Unfortunately, after Henrietta had only put a few bites into her mouth, Tara returned carrying a goblet that contained a dark red wine. Tara set the wine on the table in front of Henrietta, then took a seat across from her.

"Tell me about him," Tara said.

Henrietta swallowed the food that was in her mouth before speaking. "He's just a farmer that lived across the road from me."

"Just a farmer? I know you, Henrietta. You wouldn't drag 'just a farmer' along behind you."

"I didn't drag him. Not intentionally, at least. I haven't been able to get rid of him."

"Until now."

Henrietta nodded, then put another bite of pork into her mouth and ate it before continuing. "I'm close to my time, Tara. A couple weeks at most before I lose my life and my gift to another. I've known since I can remember how it would happen. The details have grown clearer over time, but I had always been alone when it happened."

"You saw this in a vision?"

"Yes. Every Seer knows their end."

"There's no way to avoid it?"

"I tried. I came here, first, thinking that if I wasn't where I saw the vision happen, it couldn't happen. Others can change their fate, why can't I?

"But then, you remember what happened. I left and went west, to a small town on the coast. Still, the vision never changed."

"How often do you see these visions?"

"Every few months or so. They've grown more numerous as my time grows short. I'm seeing it every few days now, if not more often."

"So your vision hasn't changed?" Tara asked.

"It did about two weeks ago, right after I met Mendleson for the first time."

"I thought you said he lived across the road from you."

"We never talked. Before I became his neighbor, his wife and child died in a fire while he was away. He has hardly been off his farm since."

"How did you end up meeting?"

Henrietta paused to eat another bite of pork and followed it up with a sip of wine. "The Fates brought us together at the local summer festival. I had a vision that showed me meeting someone there, though I couldn't see who it was. So I went. He was sitting on a bench near the area I had seen in my vision, and we struck up a conversation.

"When I went to leave, he reached for my hand and touched it. I had the vision of my end again, only this time, he was in it. I tried to run away from him, tried to change it back, but I couldn't get him to leave me alone." And then, a little softer, she said, "He just kept saving me from them."

"I don't understand," Tara said. "If he keeps saving you, why do you want him to go?"

Henrietta felt her tears start to come again, and she wiped at her eyes to forestall them, with little luck. After a moment, she gave up. "In my vision, he dies, Tara. He dies, and he still doesn't save me."

Tara stood up and stepped around the table to give Henrietta a hug. It felt good to have the comfort. It didn't stop her tears, but her muscles relaxed a bit in her friend's embrace.

"I just wish I knew why I'm crying," Henrietta said.

Henrietta felt her friend chuckle before Tara pulled away to look her in the eye. "It's obvious to me, Henrietta. I think that rope he complained about is tied to your heart. You don't really want him to go."

"That can't be it," she said. "The Fates couldn't be so cruel as to give me something like that so close to my end."

"Of course they could be so cruel. You told me long ago that it's not in the nature of the Fates to concern themselves with the fairness of their designs."

"I can't..." Henrietta began.

"You don't know what you can do. I think it's funny, in a way."

"Funny? How?"

"You've known your whole life how it would end. You've spent years preparing yourself for it. Now, they've turned your plans, whatever they may have been, upside down and you don't have any idea how to handle it."

Henrietta picked up the goblet from the table and finished off the last of the wine. She wished she had another full goblet. She'd drink that down, too. Her friend was right. It had a certain sort of humor to it. "It's a cruel joke, if you ask me."

"You don't have to let him go."

Henrietta's eyelids felt heavy. She stood up and felt the weight of her travel trying to drag her down. "I can't let him stay. I can't let him die."

"You once told me that the future is uncertain, that fates can be changed."

"Not the fate of a Seer."

"How can you be sure? You've already seen a change in your vision. How do you know it won't change more?"

Henrietta shook her head. *I'm not really considering*

letting him come along, am I? But she was. She wanted him with her. "I don't want him to die."

"Maybe he won't."

What am I thinking? I've seen it? "Tara," she said, "I appreciate your ear, but I think I'm just too tired to even think right now."

"I should stick you in his room."

"Please, no. I need time to myself."

"A room to yourself then. It's the least I can do for you. I'll put you across the hall, though, in case you decide you want to visit him."

Henrietta felt herself grimacing. She had forgotten how forward her friend could be. "Don't tell him."

Tara laughed. "I promise he'll hear nothing from me."

ELEVEN

Mendleson lay on the bed, his eyes shut against the stray rays of light that made it past the curtain's defenses, and tried to sleep. Sleep eluded him, however, as his mind wrestled with his abrupt departure from Henrietta.

He repeatedly tried to tell himself that she was right, that he was better off not helping her. If her vision was true, if his fate, were he to remain with her, meant he would die, then he would certainly be better off. He'd be alive.

But fates could be changed. She'd said so. That he was now in her vision, where he had not been before, meant that *his* fate had changed, at the very least. Of course, if he didn't go with her, that would change his fate.

And she would die.

If that was her fate, if she was supposed to die, was it his responsibility to save her? She didn't seem to want him to save her. But at times, it seemed like she had no desire to die.

His eyes popped open. "And I don't even understand why it matters to me," he said to the wood-beamed ceiling and the memory of Mirrielle. "At first, it was atonement, Mirrielle, but now? Now, I don't want to leave her, and I don't even know why."

He slammed his fist into the mattress and sat up. As tired as he was, he would never get to sleep.

He slipped out of the bed, dressed, and picked up the purse Henrietta had given him. He shoved it in a coat pocket before slipping out his door and into the hallway. He went down the stairs and into the common room, half hoping to see Henrietta, and half hoping to avoid her.

He looked around and didn't see either her or her friend Tara. He discovered that not seeing her disappointed him a little. The feeling didn't stop him, though. He went out through the door and into the streets of Berelost, hoping to walk off his restlessness.

The wind had picked up a bit while they'd been inside the inn. Alone, it wasn't enough to make him think of a storm, but a glance at the sky showed the cloud cover had grown angrier and darker. It did look like rain would begin to fall soon.

He walked, letting his feet carry him wherever they might. He didn't really see much of the city as he walked. His thoughts remained focused on his strange relationship with Henrietta and his desire to risk his life for the woman who he'd known for so short a time. He found himself wishing Paulus was along for the trip. His friend would have advice for him. He always had advice.

But talking to Paulus was impossible now. He had to figure out whether to leave Henrietta to her own devices, or not, without the help of his friend.

He chuckled quietly to himself. *It's all Paulus' fault I'm here in the first place. If Paulus hadn't dragged me to the festival that night, I'd never have met Henrietta. I'd never have touched her hand.*

After a short time, he found himself near the river again. The fishing boats had tugged at him when he and Henrietta had first come this way. He had wanted to go and visit them, visit the fisherman, see what fishing a river was like. One thought had led to another, though, and he found himself remembering the last time he'd docked his boat.

When he looked toward the boats, he expected them to be gone, but instead, he found the fishermen tying them up, lashing them tight to the docks. The water in the river looked rough, where earlier it had been fairly placid. *The wind must be whipping down that passage at a good pace.*

He looked across the river to the market and found that people were closing up shop. The square, where before it had been packed with people, had emptied. *Perhaps a storm is coming*, he thought.

He looked around one more time and decided it would be prudent to return to the inn. He hadn't come to any conclusion regarding what he should do about Henrietta, or why he was so reluctant to leave, but he didn't want to be caught out in whatever storm the citizens of Berelost thought was coming.

As he walked back to the inn, the wind pushed at him from behind. Leaflets and other bits of trash flew by him, and he picked up his pace. The storm was growing in strength almost as quickly as some of the storms that came up out on the sea where it could be sunny one moment, and an hour later, you could be hanging on to the rails of your boat for your life.

He turned the last corner before the inn, and came to a stop.

Six guardsmen stood outside its door, and a seventh man stood in front of them, issuing instructions. This seventh man, he had seen earlier that morning, and his being here could only mean that he had eventually put Henrietta's real name to her face. This time, her life hung in the balance, and her fate had nothing to do with it.

‡

Henrietta woke to the sound of someone pounding on her door. *Mendleson, why don't you just come in?*

After a moment, and a few more thumps, she realized he couldn't. She'd locked the door. She tried to blink the sleep out of her eyes. She still felt exhausted. She couldn't have been asleep long.

She wondered, as she swung her legs out from under the one blanket she'd left on the bed, how she felt about Mendleson choosing not to go. A part of her wanted to sing, but another part was still terrified of taking responsibility for his death.

"I'm coming," she said, loud enough she hoped, to be heard over the incessant banging.

She didn't have to get dressed. She had slept in her clothes.

"Ma'am!"

That's not Mendleson. "Perry?" She unlocked the door and opened it. Tara's son stood there. His eyes were wide, and he quickly glanced down the hallway toward the stairs. "What are you doing waking me up?" she asked.

"Mama told me to come get you and hurry you out the back. The magistrate is here for you."

Henrietta held onto the door as she swayed a bit. *What now? What do I do? Mendleson?* "Where's my friend?"

"He left. Mama says we have to hurry."

Left? She looked around her room and spied her pack at the end of her bed. "Where did he go?" *You weren't going to leave until tomorrow!* She left the door and went to get her pack.

"I saw him walk out the front door. I don't know where he went."

"He didn't take his horse?"

"No, Ma'am. Hurry, please!"

She slung her pack over her shoulder and raced back to the door. *Where did you go, Mendleson? Why did you leave me?*

She knew why. She'd pushed him to go. Now was not the time to cry about it.

She moved toward the stairwell, but Perry reached out and pulled at her shirt. "No, this way."

"Where?"

He started down the hallway toward the back of the inn. "We have another set of stairs back here."

Henrietta tried to think back to when she'd spent considerable time with Tara. She had never seen a staircase back here, and Tara had never mentioned it.

Henrietta followed him, and when they reached the end of the hall, Perry pulled open a closet door, and stepped inside. She entered behind him and found that it wasn't a closet door at all, but a tight set of stairs. Darkness filled the stairwell, though there was a bit of light at the bottom.

"Shut the door," said her guide.

She reached back and pulled the door closed, enveloping the top of the staircase in complete darkness. The only light was the light at the bottom.

As they descended, she kept her focus on that light, occluded now and then by Perry's bobbing head. She felt out each step with the toe of her shoe before taking it.

As they neared the bottom of the stairs, she wondered what she'd do next. Take the horse, ride east out of the city. Go home.

Home. A word, a place, she had tried not to think about in the years since she'd left. The monolith she saw in her vision, she knew it was supposed to be only a couple day's ride into the mountains.

Why am I even going home? Why am I not riding away from it?

She reached the bottom step. Perry had stepped out from the hidden staircase and around the corner, out of her sight.

She emerged into a small room. It had two doors, not counting the stairwell. One that led, she thought, into the kitchen. Another, she guessed, led out back to the stable. It was how Perry had managed to surprise her in the kitchen.

A hand reached out and gripped her arm as she took her second step into the room. She looked and found the hand was attached to a guardsman, one of the magistrates men.

"There you are, witch. You're not going that way."

She tried to pull away, but she was so tired, she barely had the strength to make the man move even a step with her.

"No, none of that. The magistrate would speak with you."

"Just let me go. I'll leave. I was only passing through on my way home."

The man laughed. "Now, I can't do that. The magistrate says to bring you to him, and that's what I'll do."

She tried to pull away again, but the guardsman's grip on her arm only strengthened, causing pain to explode from the area.

"Don't do that again, or I'll break it."

She gave up her struggle and let him drag her through the door and into the kitchen, where she found Perry in the grasp of another guardsman. She could see Perry trying to fight the man.

"Let her go," he said. "She didn't do nothing to you."

"Quiet, kid. It wasn't me she did something to. Be good, and your Momma won't get in trouble for harboring a fugitive."

Henrietta reached out and patted Perry on his head. She wanted to tell him everything would turn out fine, but she didn't believe it.

The guard marched her out through the kitchen and into the common room where the rotund magistrate stood waiting with Tara.

"There you are," said the magistrate. "Your attempt to fool me earlier didn't work, as you can see. Where is that man you were with? He's not a very good liar."

"He left."

The magistrate laughed. "Why am I not surprised?"

Henrietta wanted to reach out and hit him in his mustache, but the guardsman still held her arm tight. "Why don't you just let me go? I'm only passing through on my way home."

"You were warned to never come back. Now, here you are. You knew the consequences, yet you flouted our laws to sew more discord among our people. If I were to let you go, how can I know you just wouldn't try to return again?"

"Because I'll be dead in a couple weeks," she said under her breath.

"What?"

"I said, because I'll be dead in a couple weeks."

The magistrate's eyes lit up and he smiled. "If I have my way, you won't live even that long." He looked at the guardsman who held her. "Take her outside. I'll be there in a moment."

The guard pulled at her arm and forced her to stumble as he set out to follow the magistrates orders.

"I'm sorry," said Tara. "I..."

"It's fine, Tara. You did what you had to." And Henrietta meant it. Tara had risked her livelihood to send Perry to try to help her escape. It might still be at risk, since Perry had been caught.

The guard pulled her along and out the door into a blast of wind and a darkened sky. The first big drops of rain began to fall. She couldn't take any satisfaction in being right about the storm.

Why did I think coming back through this place would be safe? Why did I go this way?

‡

Mendleson waited inside an alcove he found and watched while the magistrate and two of his guardsmen went inside the inn. The other four stood just outside the door. He had little illusion that he could take the guardsmen by himself, but he thought if he could follow them, find out where they were taking her, he might be able to do something.

He was having trouble figuring out what that something might be.

Minutes passed while very little changed. *Maybe she's not there. Maybe she left already.* He didn't put much hope in that thought. She had to have been as tired as he was. No, she was there, and she was probably asleep. They'd find her in bed, helpless.

Unless Tara lied to the magistrate and said she wasn't there. Would Tara do something like that for her, for someone she hadn't seen in three years?

The door opened, interrupting his thought, and Henrietta stepped through it, propelled by a guard. She had her pack on her shoulder. They hadn't taken it from her.

He felt a drop of water fall on him and focused his eyes closer. It had started to rain. He hadn't noticed while he watched, but it had grown dark enough that it looked like early evening. He looked up, and saw the clouds had thickened, grown angrier, and were black with moisture.

Moments later, the magistrate walked through the

door, followed by the last guard. He had a look of glee on his face. He gave instructions, and one guardsman took Henrietta's pack while another placed her arms in shackles. The guardsmen surrounded her then, and the magistrate led them away from the inn. Their path would take them right past his alcove.

He slid back as far into the shadow as he could, hoping they wouldn't see him.

As they passed, he saw that Henrietta had her head down. *She must think I left her.* He wanted to call out to Henrietta, to tell her he was coming, but didn't. Instead, he worked furiously on a plan. He'd have to hurry, once they were out of sight.

When the procession had turned a corner, he ran out of the alcove, ignoring the rain that was now coming down even harder. Puddles were already forming where the cobblestone lay unevenly.

He burst into the common room where he found Tara standing with a look of despair in her eye.

"Mendleson," she said. "I tried to get her out, but they were too quick."

He shook his head. "It doesn't matter now. I need my pack and the horses, and something I can use for a club." A sword wouldn't be any good. He'd never trained with one. An axe would work, but he doubted they had one here.

"You're going to try to save her?"

Her question made him stop to consider, but only

for a moment. He knew what he had to do, whether it was because of his earlier need to redeem himself, or from his other surprising feelings for the Seer. "I'll do what I can," he said.

"Good. She loves you, you know."

"I'll worry about that later. I don't have any time to waste."

He ran up the stairs to get his pack. He heard Tara call out to Perry.

She loves me? He thought as he opened the door to his room. *But all she does is push me away!*

The pack was in the middle of his bed where he left it. He stared at it for a second, lost in thought. *Figure that out later, you oaf. She won't live long enough for it to matter if you don't get moving.*

He grabbed his pack, then ran out of the room and down the hallway toward the stairs and the horses. He hoped he was making the right decision. He hoped she wouldn't hate him for it.

‡

Henrietta could not remember a time when she felt more miserable than she did right at that moment. The shackles on her wrists chafed. The rain, while not seriously cold on its own, had soaked her through, allowing the beating of the wind to chill her to the bone. Her hair hung, wet and matted, into her face. Through it, she saw flashes of lightning light up the sky, followed soon after by the sound of thunder that crashed down and echoed off the walls of the city.

The guardsmen kept to a circle around her, but only touched her to push her along.

She wished she'd had visions of this moment, visions that might show her how she would escape to meet her fate at the monolith. *Please, show me a way,* she thought, but nothing came to her. She wished she had touched the hands of the guardsman that had put the shackles on her. She might have seen something that could help her.

Though, with her end so near, she might have seen nothing at all.

And with Mendleson gone, the chances of anything happening to save her were slim. *No. I'll have to figure this out for myself.*

Unbidden, a snort erupted from her. *What does it matter? I'll die either way. Why did I ever come this way?*

"We must hurry," she heard the magistrate say, though his voice sounded far off through the wind. "This storm is picking up quick."

She felt a hand push her in the back, forcing her to quicken her steps.

Another lightning flash. Thunder exploded overhead and through the streets.

She looked up and off to her left. Another lightning flash lit up the area, except for a tall, dark figure.

When the light faded, it was gone. She thought she heard one of the guards start to say something before the thunder crashed over them.

She reached up to try to brush the hair out of her face. *I saw it, right?* She proved only partially successful at clearing her face of hair, but it was enough to get a better look. She strained to look into the storm darkened streets as they walked.

Flash.

This time, two figures, walking with them.

Wraiths.

Crash. The thunder rattled her while fear settled into her belly. They had come for her again, after all this time. *Why?*

The answer eluded her. She could feel the shape of it, could touch it, even, but she was too tired and too scared.

"I've got two weeks!" she yelled.

The guard pushed her from behind, and she stumbled, only half on purpose. She fell to her knees. Anything to get the guardsmen to stop for a moment, so she could be sure, so she could figure out a way to run.

Why are they waiting?

A guard kicked her. "Get up!"

She looked up. They weren't all paying attention to her. They were looking around.

Flash!

She was looking another direction this time, and saw two more black shapes. She didn't think they were the same ones.

For a half a second, she thought she heard the sound of horseshoes striking the cobblestone. The thunder obliterated any chance of knowing for sure.

Another kick to her back, harder this time.

She stood, but not because of the kick. The time had come. She would run, if she could. *The next flash of lightning.*

She didn't have to wait that long.

"We're surrounded," she heard a guard cry out.

The guardsmen drew their long-knives and turned away from her to face the dark.

She wanted to run, now, while they were turned away, but she knew that wouldn't work. She might run right into the claws of a wraith. *Patience. Wait until they are fighting.* She could feel it coming.

The sound of horseshoes echoed down the street, unmistakeable this time.

A strong gust of wind tore through the group, almost blowing her over, and then it was time. In silence, the wraiths set upon the guards, trying to reach her, trying to retrieve the gift.

The guardsmen slashed out at the darkness, sometimes hitting their targets. Only the men screamed. One by one, they started to fall to the claws of the wraiths that they couldn't see.

Flash!

A horse bore down on her. It crashed into the melee, trampling guards and wraiths alike. She couldn't see the rider, didn't know who had come to save her, if they had come for that purpose.

The horse slowed beside her, but only slowed. A hand came down to reach for her.

Another hand reached for her from behind. A shadow of a club came down on the person, or the wraith, behind her and the hand released her.

The man on the horse was strong and pulled her up behind him with little effort. He spun the horse around and urged it to gallop down the dark, storm-washed streets.

"Thank you," she said.

"You're welcome," he said.

Mendleson. He'd come back for her. He hadn't left after all. And despite the conflict she felt over her responsibility for his impending death, she realized she was glad he had returned.

She put her head on his back and rested it there while they raced their way out of the city. It felt right.

TWELVE

Mendleson liked the feel of Henrietta's head against his back, her arms around his stomach. He wished the storm would take its leave so that he could spend his concentration on the feel of her. Instead, he pushed the horses through the gale and the sheets of water, looking to find shelter.

He didn't want to shelter too near the city for fear the magistrate had authority outside its gates. But the storm would soon force him to find shelter, he knew, or it would kill them both.

Knowing they would need both horses, if he managed to rescue her, he had asked Perry to get the other ready and wait for him to return with Henrietta. The kid had agreed without even asking for coin when he heard what Mendleson planned. He had even wanted to come along, but Tara had heard and put a stop to that nonsense.

Mendleson rode out into the storm, praying he could catch up to them before they turned off.

When he found them, his heart had stopped. They were fighting already—fighting wraiths. He kicked the horse into a gallop, pulled out the club he'd borrowed from Tara out and swung it as he crashed through the guards and the wraiths. He pulled Henrietta up onto his horse after swinging the club down onto the head of a wraith, knocking it back, then turned the horse and galloped away.

He had to keep a hold of her so that she didn't slide off. He didn't want her arms around him for fear of being hindered should he need to fight.

When they stopped at the inn to get the other horse, Henrietta refused to climb down to get on it. "I'm too tired," she said.

Instead, she put her arms up over Mendleson's head, shackles and all, then slid them down around him. He didn't protest.

They tied a lead to the other horse, and left Tara and Perry standing in the shelter of their stable.

Now, in the fury of the storm, the horses were exhausted and frightened. Every boom of thunder threatened to panic the horses and tumble he and Henrietta to the muddy ground.

When he felt they had passed beyond the immediate influence of Berelost, Mendleson started looking in earnest for a place to shelter both them and the horses.

He needed a farm with a barn or a stable, a place they could hide for the few days that Henrietta insisted the storm would assail them.

He feared the storm would kill them. He also feared that the wraiths would appear again if they stopped.

And that, more than anything, frightened him. There were more than one. The black shadows, only outlined by guttering lamps and flashes of lightning had brought the fear back to him. They'd gone so long without seeing one, he'd begun to think they'd managed to escape.

"Mendleson," Henrietta shouted over the sound of the wind. "We've got to stop. We've gone far enough." Her shout sounded strained.

Lightning, and then an immediate report of thunder caused his horse to rear and almost throw them. He dropped the lead to the other horse in his effort to not fall off, and it ran into the darkness.

Once their horse settled down, he concluded Henrietta was right. They had to stop somewhere, soon.

"The next farmhouse," he shouted, "we'll stop and ask for shelter."

He didn't hear a reply, so urged the horse onward.

A few minutes later, as they came around a bend in the road, he spied a darkened farmhouse in the distance, and rode toward it. Beside the house, he thought he saw a stable, and hoped he'd find feed for the horse, maybe hot food and a mattress for them to sleep on.

As they approached, however, he saw scorch marks around the windows in the stone walls and soon discovered that the roof had burned away. The farm was lifeless, like his own farm had been when he returned from the sea that day.

The memory rushed through him to fill every nook in his mind. The pain, the sight of Mirrielle, Josua, it all came back.

He shook his head, trying to clear it, trying to push it away, but failed. Someone had lived here in this home, and it had burned, and they were gone. They were all gone.

He kicked the horse into a gallop.

"What are you doing?" Henrietta yelled over the gale.

"I can't stay here!"

"We have to, Mendleson! We need shelter!" She sounded weak, desperate.

But the memories. He couldn't make them go away. He couldn't lock them back up in whatever box he'd managed to hide them in the last couple weeks.

"The house, it burned, just like..."

"Please, Mendleson! I need to rest."

He turned around as best he could to look at her. In the dim light the storm let through, he could see she was worn out. Her hair, normally vibrant, hung limp in the rain to cover her face. She couldn't even use her hands to brush it away, chained together as they still were around his waist. She couldn't keep her shoulders straight. She could barely even sit up, and he suspected if she wasn't chained to him, she would have fallen already.

He eyed the burnt out house once more, then took a breath and directed the horse to the stable. Whatever pain he felt at staying here, he would endure for her.

Fortunately, the disaster that fell upon the house spared the stable. The door was open, the animals gone, but the roof still held, and they were able to ride in, out of the fury of the storm.

Once inside, Mendleson slipped out from under Henrietta's arms and let himself down from the horse. He helped Henrietta down and to a nearby stool. He tied up the horse in a stall, then searched for feed. He found a bucket that had a little left in it, but it wouldn't last out the storm. He hoped it hadn't turned. He gave it to the horse anyway.

While looking for the feed, he found a ladder that led to a loft. He tried to climb it, but his legs ached from the ride, and he found himself at the end of his energy and gave up. *It can wait.*

Instead, he found the cleanest stall in the barn and brought Henrietta over to it. She slid down against a wall. He went to the horse, retrieved his pack, and brought it to the stall. He delved into it and pulled out his blanket. The oiled leather of the pack had kept it mostly dry. "At least something went right," he muttered.

Henrietta didn't even respond.

He bent down and put a hand to her cheek. She shivered under his touch.

"Come on," he said. "We have to get out of these clothes and let them dry."

"What?" she said, perking up a little. "No, just let me rest."

"No, you need to get out of them or you'll get the chills. I've got a blanket. It's dry and will keep us warm."

Her head came up so that her eyes could look at him. "Us? What are you after, Mendleson?"

"What?" he asked. "I'm not after anything but keeping us alive." He was so cold and tired, he hadn't even thought of anything else.

She looked at him, and for a moment, he thought he saw disappointment on her face. But when he looked harder, he couldn't see anything but exhaustion, and he decided it must be a trick of his mind. She'd pushed him and pushed him, and despite what Tara had told him, he saw little evidence that Henrietta had changed her mind.

"Fine," she said. "I trust you, but we have a problem." She held her hands out, and he realized immediately what it was. There was no way to get her clothes off completely while her arms were still shackled.

He looked around the stable, hoping to see a tool he could use to pop the pin or break a link in the chain, but he couldn't find anything. The stable had been stripped of most of the useful items.

He came back to her, and ultimately, they decided to remove her garments as much as possible with the shackles still on. Her top hung from the shackles, but it would at least keep the moisture away from her.

He pulled all but his underclothes off and hung them from the wall of the stall.

As he came back, he averted his eyes as best he could, and in the low light, it was easy not to see the detail of her body, but he still felt stirrings within him that he hadn't felt since Mirrielle died.

And that thought killed any of those feelings.

He stepped up next to her with the blanket, helped her to lie down on the straw covered floor, and then lay down next to her and pulled the blanket around them both. Her skin was cold and clammy on his, but his couldn't have felt much better next to her. He wrapped his arms around her to try to speed the warming.

After a while, their bodies filled the space under the blanket with enough warmth that they both stopped shivering.

"Mendleson," she said.

"What?" he asked.

"Thank you for coming to get me."

"You're welcome, Henrietta."

A warmth moved through him that had little to do with their bodies being so close together.

‡

Henrietta woke to the snapping sound of a fire. Around her, she could see the flickering light it threw off as it danced, but she couldn't see the actual fire. She began to stand up, but stopped when the shackles, and the still damp clothes hanging from them, reminded her that she only had the blanket for covering—when they reminded her of what had happened, and what hadn't.

The memories insisted that Mendleson had slept next to her, their skin touching, his warmth feeding her, the hair on his chest tickling her back, his arms holding her tight without straying where they shouldn't. But she couldn't see him.

"Mendleson?" she called out.

She heard footsteps, and then he entered the stall. He was wearing his pants, but his shirt was off. She had little choice but to admire his chest.

"You wake," he said.

"Where's your shirt?"

"Hanging by the fire with your..."

For anyone to see? She didn't yell at him for it. They did need to get them dry. "Come help me up. I want to move near the fire." *It's cold under this blanket without you to hold me.* She didn't want to say that aloud, either. She was grateful he had saved her from the magistrate and whatever fate he had planned, but she wasn't going to encourage him any further.

He bent down and very carefully helped her up. They managed to get her standing without exposing too many parts he shouldn't see. Together, they stepped out of the stall, and she saw the fire in the middle of the stable. He'd set stones in a circle to keep the fire from spreading. He had a line running across the stable, from one stall post to another, near enough to the fire to get the warmth, but not so near as to be dangerous. His shirt and coat hung from it, as well as her lower garments.

"How did you get it lit?"

"I had flints in my pack. That, straw, and a few stored pieces of wood in this place."

She sat down near the fire so that she could feel the warmth.

"How do you feel," he asked.

"Better," she said. She was still cold, but much of her fatigue had bled away while she slept. "Hungry."

Mendleson nodded and sat down next to her. He reached into his pack and pulled out a bundle of dried pork, which he handed to her. "Here, this should help."

"Where did you get this?"

"Tara stuffed it into my pack as I was leaving. She seemed to feel guilty about something."

Henrietta took a bite of it. Salty and dry, but it was better than nothing. "She felt guilty about turning me in," she said after she finished chewing.

"Turning you in?"

"She sent Perry to warn me as soon as she saw the magistrate outside, I think. But I also think once the magistrate came in, she told him where I was."

"You don't seem upset at her."

"She tried to help. It didn't work out. She couldn't risk her inn over me."

Mendleson looked up at her, his eyes dark, but bright at the same time. "I don't see why not," he said.

"You wouldn't. But then, you don't have a lot to lose, do you?" As soon as the words escaped her mouth, she wished she could take them back. The wound in his heart spilled out through his eyes before he could look away.

"I'm sorry, I didn't mean that," she said.

"What else could you mean?" He didn't look at her. "You still want me to leave. Fine. When the storm lets up, I'll leave."

Dammit, Henrietta. What do you want? She wanted to reach out to him, but the shackles made that awkward. She'd have no way to keep herself covered. "I only meant that you didn't have anything tying you to your home, that you were free to do anything. Tara, she's got Perry to think of..."

He turned back to her. "But what about my family?" Tears streamed from his eyes. "What about them? I had them."

On instinct, she withdrew her shackled hands from under the blanket, not caring that the blanket slid down, and put them over his head and around his shoulders. She pulled him close so that his head was next to hers, and she locked his gaze with hers. "They're years gone, Mendleson. You only have the memories.

You have to move on, go forward. Live your life."

"The memories eat at me," he said. "I could have saved them."

"If you had been there, could you really have saved them? Or would you be dead, too? A fire like that, in the middle of the day, they weren't asleep. If they could have escaped, they would have. You would have been trapped, too, or you would have watched helplessly."

"But..."

"You were out at sea, Mendleson, where you were supposed to be. It wasn't your fault. You have to move on."

The tears had stopped, but his eyes were still moist. His breath on her was warm. She had a sudden urge to lean forward and kiss him, but she resisted. She had no idea what he'd think.

"I'm trying to let them go. I'm trying to leave that all behind. It's why I'm still here even though you keep pushing me away."

"I thought you were here because you were trying to save me to atone for how you think you failed your family."

He didn't say anything for a moment. She thought maybe she'd said the wrong thing again. Then he said, "I was."

"I don't understand."

"At first, you were right. I thought I might atone for my failure if I saved you. But then, after the second, or maybe the third time, it became..." He stopped, and then looked down.

She grew acutely aware that the blanket had fallen away to expose her breasts, but she ignored the urge to try to cover herself. "What did it become?" she asked.

His eyes came up to meet hers again. "Tara told me that you love me. Is that true?" he asked.

What? Tara told him? Is it true? Her heart fluttered in her chest. She didn't know how to answer the question. "What did it become, Mendleson?"

He moved a little closer. Their noses were almost touching. "You keep pushing me to leave, to save myself from you."

It's true, but not any more. "You keep saying that. Tell me why you continue to stay with me."

"It became about saving you for me."

Her heart split She pulled her hands from his shoulders and put them on his head and pulled his lips to hers. They were rough from the weather, but so warm. He seemed to want to pull away at first, but a moment later, the tension in him evaporated. His tongue probed at her lips. She let her tongue meet his, and it was so soft, gentle, yet strong. She had imagined kissing a man for most of her life, yet had never imagined this.

He put his arms around her and pulled her tight to him, so that her breasts were against his chest. The hair tickled her nipples at first, and then she forgot about it in the depths of their kiss.

Time passed, she didn't know how much, and then

their lips parted. Neither of them said a word for long moments as they stared into each other's eyes. He seemed to be waiting for something.

"I don't know what love is," she said. "But I do know that I don't want you to leave."

"Good. I'm not leaving," he said.

"But my vision, my fate, your fate. If you stay with me, you'll die. I don't want that either."

"Henrietta. You've seen how I am just thinking about Mirrielle. How do you think I'll be if I let you go, too? We'll find a way. You can always change someone's fate. The fact that I'm now tied to yours only proves that yours can be changed. Why do we even have to go to that place? Why can't we go somewhere else?"

At his question, the part she'd been missing, the idea that she had just been able to touch while the guardsmen had her, finally took shape in her mind.

"Mendleson, we can't go anywhere else."

"Why not?"

"The wraiths only appear when I am not on the path to my fate. As long as I move toward it, they leave me alone."

He leaned in to her again and gave her a tender kiss. "We'll find a way," he said. "I won't let you die."

THIRTEEN

Mendleson lifted Henrietta's arms over his head and pulled away from their embrace. It felt good to get rid of the cold damp from the clothes that were still stuck on her shackles, but he missed the closeness of her almost immediately. He got one last peek at her breasts before she covered herself with the blanket again. He could still feel them against his chest. It had been a long time since he'd been that close to a woman.

"What do we do now?" Henrietta asked.

He looked at her wrists where they held the blanket up close to her. In the orange of the firelight, it was hard to tell, but they looked like they were starting to rub raw.

"I think we need to find a way to get those shackles off of you. I wish we had the key." He stood up.

He almost felt dizzy. His mind raced in at least three directions. How to save her from her fate, how to get the shackles off, and how to get that close to her again. But for the last, those shackles had to come off.

"How do we get them off?"

"If there was a forge here, with tools, I could get them off. But the tools are gone, and I haven't looked outside to see if they had a forge."

"Couldn't you just pick the lock on them?"

Mendleson laughed. "Of course." *What can I use?* He bent down to his pack and rummaged through it. The blade of his knife was too big to fit. Everything else, flints, extra clothes, was useless for the job. He looked around the stable, but he'd already searched most of it. Whatever had been of use here had already been taken.

"What about nails?"

That kiss must have addled my brain. "Good thought. There should be some around here." *Unless they shod the horses elsewhere.*

A quick search of the stable turned up three nails of different sizes. There were probably more, but he thought he'd give the three he'd found a try first.

He sat down next to her, and she laid her hands in his lap. He turned the shackle on her right hand so that the keyhole was visible to him, and then he went to work with the nails. After several minutes of fiddling, he managed to slip the nail into the mechanism so that the bar of the shackle popped free.

Henrietta immediately pulled her hand free and used the other to rub at the wrist. "That feels so much better," she said.

"Let me see the other."

She gave it to him and it went much quicker this time. In only a minute, he got that one to pop open also. She rubbed at her wrist a bit, then reached over and hugged him properly. "Thank you," she said into his ear.

The blanket started to slip down again, but she stopped it with one of her newly freed hands and sat back.

Mendleson fished the shackles out of her clothes, then hung her clothes up on the line next to his own. When that was done, he patted his own shirt and found it dry. He put it on. Away from the fire, and away from Henrietta, the stable was still cold.

"What are you doing?" she asked.

"I've been thinking about what you said, about the need to move on." He had only just started thinking about it since he stood up, but he wasn't going to tell her that. "I think I'm going to go look over that house."

"You're going out? In this storm?"

With everything that had happened, he'd nearly forgotten the storm. He had still heard the wind, the rain on the roof, the drips where it leaked into the stable, but the closed door had kept most of it out and Henrietta had kept his mind occupied. "Yes. I won't go far. I need to look at it. I need to confront the memories. I think you're right."

"Do you want me to come with you?"

He shook his head. "No, I think I should do this on my own. You stay here, tend the fire. Check on the horse and see if you can find more oats or something for him to eat."

She looked up at him with big eyes that reflected the firelight. "Don't be long," she said.

"I won't be," he said as he turned and went to the stable door.

He opened the door a crack. Wind and water rushed in. He slipped through the opening and shut the door behind him. Within moments, he was soaked and chilled. He thought about putting this off until the storm stopped, but for the first time, he wanted to be free of the pain his memories had given him for the last four years. He wanted to be able to give himself completely to Henrietta, now that she would no longer try make him leave.

He hunched over as he walked the distance between the stable and the house. He had to negotiate the soup of mud that the stable yard had become. It sucked at his feet and made the going slow.

The burnt out house loomed in front of him, and the memories of his own home, the smoke rising from its shell, the cinders falling from the air, came back to him. He made his way to where the door of the building used to be. A stone arch surrounded it.

A strong gust of wind blew and pushed him sideways, but he refused to let it knock him over.

He stepped through the arch. Inside the stone, there was little left. Burnt timber, the broken bones of the house, lay where it had fallen, spread out on a stone floor. Fired pots lay smashed and shattered among the wreckage of the house. He stepped over each shattered bone with reluctance, expecting to see the charred bodies of his wife and son as they were when he'd found them, Mirrielle clutching Josua in a final, protective embrace.

But he never did see them. They weren't here. This wasn't his house. It wasn't his life. He looked up into the rain falling from the cloud blackened sky and let the drops fall on his face. The wind couldn't move him. The rain couldn't beat him down.

He reached back to that day, when his boat sailed into the harbor, its belly full of fish. He'd seen the smoke. He'd known, even then. He realized, as the rain pounded on him, that he'd lost two loves that day: his family and the sea. The one would never come back, not as it was, and it wasn't his fault.

"It wasn't my fault!" he shouted into the fury of the storm.

But the other, the sea, he had given that up to tend his memories. *I gave up the sea for something that was already gone.*

He thought of Henrietta, back in the stable, waiting for him. *Am I doing it again? Am I giving up my life for something I can't have?*

That he even asked the question bothered him. He pulled his eyes from the sky, wiped them free of water, and looked around the house. It was empty, burnt out, ruined. *There are no ghosts here to answer my questions.*

Off in the corner, where the kitchen might have been, he saw something on the floor. A ring of iron. A panel of wood that was charred but not burnt through. A large beam lay atop it. He ran over to it, and saw that with some effort, he might be able to move the beam.

It was an answer, of sorts.

‡

When the door opened again, a blast of cool air caused the small fire to sputter. Henrietta had to dive for her blanket to cover up. She made it just before Mendleson stepped through the door carrying a large, nearly full, burlap sack. He shut the door behind him, and the fire returned to its natural dancing self.

"Look what I found," Mendleson said as he came to the fire bearing his burden.

As he approached, the light of the fire showed his clothes covered in soot and charcoal. His hands were black with it, too. "What were you doing?"

"The place had a cellar filled with food. Much of it spoiled, but there were still some treasures. Salted meats, and a bunch of potatoes that don't look too bad."

"But you're covered in soot."

"A large beam had fallen across the cellar door. I had to lever it out of the way."

"Let me see what you found, while you dry yourself and change."

He handed the sack to her, and then started to strip off his clothing. She looked through the treasure he had found. It wasn't a lot, and in the light of the fire, she could see a few of the things he had found had spoiled more than he thought. However, there was enough to last through the storm for them, if they were careful.

"I wish there was a pot to cook these potatoes in," she said.

"Look in the bottom," he said.

She looked up from the sack for a moment and saw him kneeling at his pack, naked but for his small clothes. She admired his shoulders and chest for a moment, until she saw his hands again, still covered in soot.

"Go wash your hands," she said.

"Huh?"

"Go outside and wash those hands before you get your other clothes dirty."

He looked at his hands and grinned. "Right." He left for the door, and she watched him walk away. The farm work had been good to him.

She pulled her eyes from him and delved into the bottom of the sack. She reached a hand down to the bottom and found, to her delight, an iron pot. The idea of hot potato soup warmed her stomach without having even cooked it yet.

She had found a workbench in the corner while Mendleson was away. She took the sack over to it and emptied its contents onto the bench, setting things in order as she did. Once that was taken care of, she went back to Mendleson's pack for his knife. She stopped by her clothes and tested her blouse. It was still damp. *It would be so much easier to cook without this blanket.*

Mendleson came back in, his hands, and most of the rest of him, clean. This time, she got to admire the front. And then she thought of the pot.

"I saw a well outside," she said.

"Let me guess," he said.

She ran to the bench to get the pot. She took it to Mendleson, and he sighed. Henrietta laughed. "You're not even going to ask me what I want?" she asked.

"I know already," he said, taking hold of the pot and turning back to the door.

She went back to her makeshift kitchen and began to slice up the potatoes. She looked at the other things he'd brought and decided adding salted beef might flavor the soup a bit. She cut up a portion of the beef into tiny bits. Enough to flavor, but not enough that they'd run out before the storm abated.

She turned around when the door opened again and saw Mendleson enter with the pot of water. She smiled. It looked like he'd also managed to find a couple metal rods that might serve to hold the pot off the fire. For a moment, she wondered at her earlier desire to make him leave. Of course, thinking that brought the vision to her mind, her fate, and now his. Her smile faded.

He brought the pot to her and set it on the bench. She shoveled the potatoes and meat into it while he went to the fire and worked the rocks around to support the metal rods.

She carried the pot to the firepit and the blanket gaped open, but she decided to ignore it. Mendleson was practically naked, and he'd already seen her. He'd already lain next to her, their skin touching.

She felt her skin flush as she thought of it and hoped he didn't see. She looked up at him, but he wasn't watching. He was using a piece of cloth he'd found somewhere to dry himself.

She set the pot on the bars, then sat down in front of the fire and closed the blanket around her. She watched him dress, and found herself wishing he wouldn't.

"The other thing you were doing at the house," she said. "How did that go?" She wasn't sure what she wanted to hear.

He finished putting his clothes on and sat down next to her before answering.

"I'm not sure how to answer," he said. "I still feel a hole within me that I don't think can ever be filled. It hurts."

She found herself holding her breath.

"But I think I know now that you are right, that Paulus was right. It's time to stop blaming myself for it. It's time to stop punishing myself."

She let her breath out. *Please don't say that you're leaving.* "When I was young," she said, "having just come into my sight, I would see things, and then they would happen. For the longest time, I remember thinking that what happened was my fault. No matter how many times my grandmother told me that it was not my fault, I couldn't believe her."

"How old were you?"

"I came into my sight when I was six."

"You couldn't know," he said.

"You're right. I couldn't. I had to learn. But a couple years passed, I think, before I had a vision and saw a future that didn't happen." She looked away from him and into the fire.

"What was it?" he asked.

"A friend of mine, a young boy. I saw him crushed under falling rocks. There is a cliff near where I grew up. A lot of the children liked to try to climb it. That's what I saw him doing in my vision.

"So I told him... I told him to do anything else in the world, but please don't go climbing the cliff." Talking about the memory brought back the hurt that she had buried so long ago.

"And he did, didn't he."

She nodded. "He stayed away from the cliff face. The rocks fell, just as I saw in my vision, but no one was hurt.

"That day, he chose to go swimming in the river. He lost his footing, his head hit a rock and split open, and he drowned."

"You must have hated yourself."

She reached out and stirred the soup with Mendleson's knife. "For a while, I think I did. But I was confused. I believed what my grandmother said about the visions I had before that one—the ones where I did not intervene. Those weren't my fault. But after my friend died, I had to decide if I was responsible.

"It's the basic philosophical problem that all Seers face. Do you tell the subject of your vision about the bad things so that they can avoid them? Do you encourage other actions? If something happens because of those other actions, are they your fault? If you don't tell the person, do you share responsibility for what happens to them?"

"Is there a right answer?"

She shook her head. "I don't know. My grandmother told me I had no responsibility for the visions, but I had a responsibility for what I did with them. I decided that my responsibility extended only to telling the subject what my vision of their future was, and that the choice of what to do with their knowledge was their own."

They sat in silence together for a moment. The wind outside, and the lesser sound of the crackling fire were the only things she heard.

"If that's what you decided, why did you keep pushing me away?"

"I don't want you to die, Mendleson. Not for me. For the longest time, there was no one in my vision but me, and then we touched at the festival and you were in it. Somehow, I had changed your future. I am responsible for you being here."

He moved closer to her and put his arm out, as if he would put it around her. She leaned into him, and he did put his arm around her shoulders. It felt good, and comforting.

"I don't believe you are responsible for my being here. My actions are my own, and you've said yourself that fates *can* be changed. That I'm here is proof of it.

"And if you think about it, if we can't really change our ultimate fate, perhaps the Fates manipulated you into meeting me. Couldn't they have left me out of your vision so that you would try to change your fate and take your journey to find me? Didn't you say that you had a vision where you saw yourself meeting someone at the festival?"

She nodded. *Could it be possible? Was I supposed to find him? Have I ever been given the complete vision at any time before I met him? Do I even have it now?*

She stirred the pot a bit more and decided it was done. She would reserve those thoughts for another time.

She remembered their bowls had been in her pack. "Did you happen to find bowls on your search?"

"No," he said, but he reached into his pack and pulled out a spoon. "I'll share my spoon, though."

She laughed. "It's going to take us a long time to finish this soup."

He put his hand to his ear and made a show of listening to the storm. "We've got time."

Yes, she thought. *But how much?*

FOURTEEN

The storm raged on another two days. Mendleson was more than happy to spend the time with Henrietta, huddled around the fire, keeping warm. She'd put her clothes on once they were dry enough, and he lamented silently that she had done so. They never quite approached each other so intimately during those days as they had the first night and morning, and he yearned for another kiss.

But they each had their vulnerabilities, and they tiptoed around them while they talked. She didn't push him away, like she had before, but she didn't bring him closer, and he feared to push too much lest she change her mind. He satisfied himself with the little touches: putting his arm around her, rubbing her back, sharing their one spoon.

He'd gone looking for other utensils in the house, but could find nothing left that was useful. Anything that had survived the fire had been taken.

On the third day of their stay in the stable, the rain let up, and the wind ceased to howl. He peaked outside and found that, while the sky was still filled with clouds, they had grown light and thin.

"Do you think we should wait a day for the road to dry up some?" he had asked.

She shook her head. "I don't think that would be a good idea. The wraiths seem to stay away if we are moving toward the monolith." He knew she was thinking of her vision. "I don't know if they will hold off another day."

So they let the horse graze on what he could find while they packed their few things into Mendleson's pack. They still had a bit of salted beef left, and they packed that too. When the sun had risen to its highest point, they set off, once again, toward the fate Henrietta envisioned for them.

The road turned out to be fairly solid, despite all the rain. There was a layer of mud on top, but it was only a few inches thick. Mendleson dug down at one point and found a layer of stone underneath. It had been paved at one point, long ago.

They took turns riding the horse. They didn't want to tire him, in case they needed to ride quickly.

They didn't bother to travel at night anymore, either. Henrietta expressed enough confidence in her theory that the wraiths would not harm her as long as she was moving toward her fate that Mendleson agreed when she said she'd prefer to travel when she could see.

The next day, Mendleson caught his first glimpse of the mountains where, if Henrietta was right, they would meet their end. Mendleson still thought there should be a way to change it, and he kept trying to get Henrietta to work with him at trying to find a way, but every time he came up with an idea, she pointed out why it wouldn't work.

As they grew closer and closer to the mountains, Mendleson found himself growing more and more worried. Whatever had happened between them in the stable seemed less and less real. Their impending doom cast a shadow that Mendleson believed had come to dominate Henrietta's thoughts. As the miles disappeared behind them, Henrietta spoke fewer and fewer words, and would not talk about what was ahead of them at all.

By the time they rode into Tearing Falls, three days later, Henrietta had not made a sound for hours.

FIFTEEN

Mendleson was leading the horse, and Henrietta was riding it, when they entered a small town at the foot of the mountains. A small decrepit sign declared the name of the place in burnt script to be "Tearing Falls". Dusk was upon them, and it would not be long before they would need to find shelter.

All of the buildings had stone walls and wore steep roofs covered in wood shingles. They lined the road like they were watching a parade. Children played in the street, despite the late hour. Men and women strolled the road, directing guarded looks toward the two strangers.

"Have you been here before?" Mendleson asked Henrietta.

"Years ago," she said, but she didn't elaborate.

"Is there an inn or somewhere else we can stay?"

She said nothing for a while, but just about the time Mendleson was going to try and ask someone, she said,

MARK FASSETT

"There's someone at the far end of the town that might take us in, if he still lives here."

Mendleson looked up at her and found her staring off into the distance, up somewhere into the darkening mountains.

Mendleson led the horse on through the town. It didn't take them long to get through it. Mendleson guessed fewer than a hundred people lived nearby.

When they reached the far edge of the town, Henrietta pointed him toward a home that was a bit larger than the rest of them.

"Who lives here?" he asked.

She didn't have time to answer before the door to the house opened and an older man stepped out, his balding head bare to the night air.

"Henrietta," he said. "Good to see you."

Mendleson saw as the man walked toward them that, despite his age, the old man was still in strong health. He stood straight, his shoulders back, his arms still wrapped with muscle.

"Hello, uncle," she said. "Do you think we might stay the night?"

"Of course," he said as he reached up to help his niece from the horse. When Henrietta was down, he gave her a big hug. "I haven't seen you through here in years. I thought you had..."

"Not yet uncle. Not yet, but soon."

He gave her a more tender hug. Mendleson realized her uncle knew about her future.

"It's a shame it must come so soon," her uncle said. Then he stepped back and turned to Mendleson. "Are you going to introduce me to this man you're with, or do I need to run him off."

She laughed, a sound Mendleson hadn't heard in days. "You don't need to run him off. Uncle, this is Mendleson. He's my..." She stopped.

"Your what?" He stepped over and shook Mendleson's hand, clapped him on the back, and pulled him close. His grip was strong enough, Mendleson wouldn't have been able to resist. "I don't care what you are," he said. "If you hurt her, you'll have to answer to me."

"I'm actually hoping to prevent any hurt to her," Mendleson said.

Her uncle clapped him on the back one more time. "Good. I'm Karl. Nice to meet you." Then Karl stepped back. "Give me the horse and I'll stable him. You two head inside and get cleaned up. You look like you've had a long road."

Mendleson handed him the reins, took his pack from the horse, and followed Henrietta through the open door.

Inside, the home looked well kept. It had a front room that shared a kitchen area. A painting hung on one stone wall, and a pair of swords held a place on the mantle above the fireplace.

"Come," Henrietta said. "Follow me."

She led him through a door at the back of the room

that opened into a short hallway. She led him to the end, past a pair of opposing doors, where he found a third door. She opened it and they entered a small room that had a tub. It had a water pump.

"A well inside the home?" he asked.

"The well used to be outside, but in the winter, it gets cold enough that my Uncle decided to build a room around it. The house grew from there."

She started pumping water into the tub. Mendleson tested it and found it nearly ice cold.

"You're going to get in there?" he asked.

"No. This is for you. I'm going to talk to my Uncle while you clean up. You smell like a pig."

He put his hand in the water again. "I'll freeze."

"Look behind you. There are washrags on the shelf. Just wipe yourself with them."

She stopped pumping, then squeezed around him so that she could leave. He'd almost forgotten what it felt like to have her touch him.

"Don't take long," she said, and then she left.

Mendleson kept watching, hoping she might poke her head back in. When she didn't, he stripped off his clothes and resigned himself to another cold bath.

‡

She was sitting in one of her uncle's soft chairs, resting, when her uncle came in from stabling the horse.

"You're not cleaning up?"

"Mendleson is going first. I'd hoped you could start the fire so I could have a warm bath."

He laughed. "Of course. You're going to make him suffer the cold?"

Henrietta smiled. "I guess it isn't very nice, but he has a musk about him right now that needs removing."

He sat down across from her. "So tell me why you are here. I had thought you left so that you might avert your fate, that you might change your vision."

"I did. I didn't intend to come back, but I think the fates have conspired against me. Everything I do leads me back."

"Your grandmother told you this might happen."

"I know. But she... she lived so long with her sight. Why am I given so little time?"

"Hen, that's not for us to know. You know that."

She couldn't respond to that in any way that didn't sound like she was a little girl again. "I met someone who told me that there might be a way."

"A way?"

"A way to avoid my fate. She told me of the Oracle of Arabeth."

Her uncle sat back in his chair and rubbed at his bald pate for long moments without saying anything.

"Do you know of her? It sounds like she might be a Seer, too."

He sat forward, and leaned toward her. "Look at me. That woman is no Seer. I've heard a great many strange tales about her. Some say that she's been hidden up in the mountains for hundreds of years, that she's not even human. It is not safe to go to her."

"Uncle, how can it be any less safe than my current fate?"

He sighed. "I don't know. I only know that the help she offers is supposed to carry a price that is often heavier than the petitioner is able to bear."

A silence hung between them, until he said, "Even if I knew where she could be found, I wouldn't send you to her."

And then he stood, looking weary for the first time. Henrietta suspected he knew more than he was telling, but she knew once her uncle decided something, it stayed decided.

"I'm going to get some wood for your fire." He walked out and left her staring into the empty hearth. *If he won't tell me how to find the Oracle, did I come all this way for nothing? Did I drag Mendleson this far to die?*

And when she thought of him, all of her worry that she'd been feeling since they left the safety of the stable came to her. She knew he was confused because she had stopped talking to him, stopped touching him, and erected a barrier that he hadn't been able to scale. But she'd decided that, even if he would come along, and even though she wanted him with her more than just about anything else, she wouldn't be a party to his death. She wouldn't encourage him in any way.

If only the sight of him didn't make my mind lose all semblance of reason.

But if I can't find the Oracle, what then? Will all of it be for nothing?

When Mendleson emerged from the short hallway and interrupted her thinking, she almost smiled before she remembered herself. He had even shaved the beard he had grown over the last two weeks. She wanted to go to him and touch his face.

No. Not until I know he's safe.

SIXTEEN

Mendleson felt put out when he discovered he could have had a warm bath instead of the practically ice cold wash-down he had suffered through. He didn't understand. Back at the stable, she had been so warm and comfortable to be around. Now, while she wasn't pushing him away like she had before, she wasn't letting him close to her, either.

While Henrietta took her bath, Karl gave him a mug of mead to sip at, and then left Mendleson to sit by the fire that was now burning in the hearth while Karl prepared a meal. Mendleson had asked if Karl needed help, but Karl declined any assistance. It didn't stop Karl from striking up a conversation, though.

"Mendleson, how did you meet my niece?" Karl asked.

"She lived across the road for about three years."

"But that's not how you met her."

Mendleson took a sip of his mead. "No. The town

festival, three, maybe four weeks ago. She came over to me. We struck up a conversation."

"Did she say why she came over to you?"

"Not then, no. But later, she told me she'd had a vision of herself meeting someone there."

"You?" Karl asked.

"She never said."

"It must be you, if she didn't meet anyone else."

"How can you be sure?"

Karl laughed. "Has she not told you of me?"

"No. She never mentioned you."

"Strange." Mendleson heard Karl stirring something in a metal pot. "Well, I can be sure because my wife was a Seer, as was Hen's grandmother. It sort of runs in the family."

"Your wife?"

"Henrietta's aunt."

Mendleson stood up and went to stand next to Karl. "She's not here?"

"She passed away at the same time Henrietta's mother did. They were close."

"I'm sorry."

"No need to be sorry. It was a long time ago, and we knew it was coming. I've made my peace with it."

"If you don't mind my asking, how long did that take?"

"Years." Karl turned to look at him. "Why do you ask?"

Mendleson peered into the boiling pot, avoiding the Karl's eyes. "My wife and child died in a fire. It still..." He trailed off. He'd thought the pain would go away after he had disavowed responsibility, but it still lingered.

"Yes," Karl said. "It still hurts. And it will. It's no easy thing to lose your love."

They stood in silence while Karl stirred the stew.

"Enough of this talk. I've banned melancholy from my life. Tell me, how did Hen manage to drag you along on this trip." His voice hadn't regained much of its enthusiasm.

"She didn't drag me along. Not on purpose, at least. Something happened, I touched her hand on accident while we were talking at the festival, and she pulled away from me and fell. She got up and ran away."

"She had a vision."

Mendleson nodded. "I didn't know it at the time. I thought I had offended her. When I went to apologize, I found a wraith at her door, trying to kill her."

Karl's eyes widened and he stopped stirring the stew. "She's closer than I thought."

"I stopped it and made her take me along. I wanted to protect her. I didn't want to let another woman die because of my inaction."

"You can't stop it, son. Hen's time is her time."

"Trust me, I know."

"I don't believe you do. Hen's mother tried to help my wife. They both died."

Mendleson heard footsteps behind them. "That's not what you told me, Uncle. That's not what Gran said."

Karl and Mendleson turned to face her at the same time. Henrietta was cleaner than he had seen her in weeks. Her hair had become silk again, her face had lost the smudge marks. But her brow was furled, her jaw set.

Karl took a short breath, then said, "You were so young, Hen. We didn't want you to be afraid of your gift any more than you already were. You blamed yourself for the things that happened in your visions. We didn't want to add the death of your mother onto that burden."

"It might have changed some things if I had known." She looked at Mendleson.

"I don't think so, Hen. It can't be changed. Your mother tried. No matter how many of those things they fought off, there were always more."

"Why didn't you help them?"

"I tried, at first."

"And then you gave up?"

"What was I supposed to do? They just kept appearing. Night after night. More and more of them."

Mendleson could feel the anger, frustration, and pain radiating from Henrietta, and he understood it. She seemed to recognize it, too. She looked at him, caught his eye. *I'll never stop, Henrietta,* he thought at her. He hoped she could hear it, or at least feel it. He didn't want to say it aloud. Karl didn't know about Henrietta's vision, and now did not seem the best time to bring it up.

Karl turned back to his stew, apparently unable to

face Henrietta any longer. He stirred the pot a bit, and then said, "It's done. Perhaps some food will help us all calm down."

Mendleson didn't think food would help at all.

‡

Henrietta tried to decide who she held more anger for: her uncle, or her grandmother. In the dark of the night, alone in her uncle's bed, she pondered whose offense was worse, and could not come to a conclusion. All she could think was that her grandmother, long dead, was beyond her reach, and her uncle was asleep in a chair in the front room.

Her uncle had given her his room and Mendleson the other room. Mendleson looked like he wanted to argue against it, but after learning what happened to her mother, she didn't want her uncle to know how close she felt to Mendleson.

She had two minds on that topic, as well. She wanted him to leave on his own, she wanted him to decide it wasn't worth it, and she wanted him to decide to save himself. He deserved to live, to find love somewhere else where that love wouldn't die in a week. After all the pain he had suffered, he deserved better.

But, she also wanted him to stay, to protect her, to sleep beside her like they had in the barn. She wanted more touches, another kiss. She craved them every night since, but the vision stopped her. If she gave in to her desires, she knew there would be no way to save him.

What was worse, she suspected her uncle knew how to find the Oracle. She only wished she knew why he wouldn't tell her.

Her options were growing few in number, if indeed she'd ever had many options. She wanted to talk to someone about them. She wanted to talk to Mendleson about them. They hadn't been able to talk over supper. Despite her uncles hopes, there was too much tension, mostly from her anger. Few words were spoken at all.

The idea of sneaking into Mendleson's room and laying down next to him crept into her mind. It excited her, and she sat up in her bed.

"No, Henrietta," she said. "If you go, you go to talk. Not to lay next to him."

She ran her hands down along her body over the nightgown her uncle had given her, and imagined they were Mendleson's hands.

She stopped herself. "No. Just to talk. To figure out what to do next."

Henrietta reached over, and turned up the lamp a bit so she could see. She swung herself out of bed and crossed the room to the door. She pulled it open with care. She didn't want her uncle to hear, though with the amount of mead he had consumed after supper, she thought he might not wake to an earthquake.

The door at the end of the hall was shut, the hallway

dark. She stepped across the hallway, her bare feet making little sound, and tried the handle on the door. It was unlatched.

She opened it and stepped through, shutting the door behind her.

"Who's there?" Mendleson's asked from somewhere in the dark.

"Henrietta," she said.

"What are you doing here?" he asked.

"I need to talk." *I need you to touch me.*

"What about? You should be sleeping. We have a long day tomorrow."

She moved toward the bed. "That's what I wanted to talk about. Do you mind if I climb under the covers with you? It's cold out here." *What am I doing? I'm just going to talk, get answers.* But her body wanted more, and she could feel it.

She heard him move in the bed. "Climb in," he said. He sounded nervous. She wished she could see his face in the dark, but all she could make out was a vague shadow.

She slipped in next to him, and felt his warmth. Her hand accidentally came to rest on his chest. She left it there.

"What are we talking about," he asked.

"My uncle. I think he knows how to find the Oracle, but he won't tell me." Her fingers idly traced a pattern in the hair on his chest.

"Why won't he tell you?"

"He fed me a story about how she requires payments for her advice that are often greater than the advice is worth. It seems he thinks she is a witch or something."

Mendleson rolled to face her, even though they could not really see each other in the dark. Her hand fell from his chest, but she made sure it was still touching him.

"If he won't tell us, then we'll have to find someone who will. There's got to be someone else around here who knows."

His hand idly took hers and rubbed it.

In front of them, stood a monolith. Ancient and implacable. She walked toward it, but Mendleson pulled away. He looked around in a terrified movement. He pulled out his knife.

The wraiths descended on him like a flock of crows on carrion. Soon, he was smothered, and she could not see him. Her feet were stuck to the ground. She couldn't move. The wraiths stood, leaving Mendleson's body crumpled on the ground, the life gone from it.

They came toward her. She backed up, and backed up, until her back came to rest against the monolith.

The wraiths spread out around her. Trapped. They closed in, until she could no longer see anything but their hungry eyes.

"I'm sorry, I'm sorry," she heard him say as she came out of the vision.

"No, don't be sorry."

"But I know it's painful for you."

"No," she said, trying to comfort him. "I've seen it so many times. I just don't like seeing you…"

She reached out and put her arm around him, careful not to touch his hand with hers again. "Come close," she said.

"But…"

And then, with him so close to her, she decided she wanted to know, had to know, before the Fates brought her end. For the moment, she didn't care what Mendleson would think. They hadn't been able to change that vision. Not yet.

She pulled his head to hers and kissed him. This time, their bodies were warm, and she could feel him along the length of her body. She wanted the nightgown off.

She pulled her mouth from his. Her heart raced. She didn't know if she was doing the right thing, but it felt right. Her body wanted it, ached for it. "I want to lay with you, at least once," she whispered to him. "I want to know what it would have been like."

"But you've been so distant these last few days." He sounded confused.

She moved her hand down his back. She felt his creep tentatively on to her hip. "I'm sorry," she said. "I've just been confused—afraid."

"What changed?"

"Please, Mendleson. Isn't this what you want?"

She slipped her hand farther down, and discovered

he wasn't wearing anything at all. She pulled herself closer to him, so that she could feel his hardness against her.

His tentative touch grew stronger, slipped around to her backside, and he pulled her tight to his body. His mouth came down on hers again, insistent and probing. His free hand tangled itself in her hair. Her body tingled in anticipation.

His hand on her backside started pulling the night-gown up. She lifted her body a bit from the bed to help him, while their tongues still explored each other's warmth.

Their lips parted for a moment as the hem of her nightgown slipped past her hips, and the hard length of him had unhindered access to her.

"I do want this," he said.

She brought his head back down to hers. He slipped his fingers down from her nightgown, slipped them between her legs. She opened herself to them, and they touched her gently, and rubbed until she felt her moisture come through and his fingers grow wet.

Then, he rolled her onto her back, put himself between her legs, and slowly slid himself into her. At first, she felt pain, and she wondered for a bit if it would last, but she soon forgot it as he moved within her and other sensations spread throughout her body.

They moved against each other, and she grasped him, pulled him deep into her, again and again, until lights flashed through her mind and her body spasmed like nothing she had ever felt before. She almost didn't feel his own spasms through the sea of pleasure that enveloped her.

He came to a rest on her, his body somehow not crushing her beneath it.

She held him close when it seemed he would roll off. She wanted him to stay there forever.

But she knew it wouldn't last, and probably wouldn't happen again.

And then she allowed him to roll off, and they both lay there gasping for a moment.

Tears came to her, and she had to choke them off. She couldn't let him throw away his life for her. *I have to do something.*

She slipped out of the bed.

"Where are you going?"

"Back to my bed. I don't want Uncle to find me here. It's best he not know, I think."

"Right," Mendleson said. He sounded disappointed. "I'll see you in the morning, then."

"Goodnight," she said.

"Goodnight."

She went through the door and shut it behind her before she whispered, "Goodbye, Mendleson."

‡

"Mendleson! Help!"

At first, he thought the words were part of his dream, the nightmare that he slipped into after Henrietta left his room and he fell asleep.

He had felt so good after she had opened to him. He hadn't wanted her to leave, but he understood. After what she had learned from her uncle about her mother's death, she hadn't wanted to tell him anything more about the relationship between her and Mendleson. When Karl had tried to probe, Henrietta shut him down every time. Mendleson couldn't tell if she was angrier at him for lying about her mother, or for not helping her. Mendleson had come to the conclusion that, despite the man's strong appearance, he was a bit of a coward.

And then the dream came as he slipped into sleep. Henrietta running, then laying on the ground, then Henrietta limp in his arms while he searched through a dark forest for something he couldn't find.

"Mendleson! They're here!"

He woke.

"Mendleson! Uncle!"

Henrietta's voice, screaming.

Mendleson fell out of bed, then raced for his door. Instinctively, he knew why she was screaming. The wraiths had come for her.

He yanked the door open and looked down the hallway. He couldn't see anything.

But why did they come for her? We were going

where they wanted!

He ran across the hall and opened her door. There was no one inside.

"Help!"

That sounded like it was coming from outside.

The hallway door that led to the front room opened, and Mendleson saw Karl standing there looking at him.

"She's not here. I think she's outside," Mendleson said.

"Fool girl." Karl ran back into the front room, and Mendleson chased after, ignoring his nakedness.

He ran into the room to find Karl pulling the swords from the Mantel. He looked Mendleson up and down once, but said nothing and handed one of the swords to him. "Do you know how to use that?"

Mendleson shook his head.

"Well, don't stab me with it. Come on."

Karl led Mendleson out the front door. It was cool outside, but not nearly as cool as it had been during the storm.

Mendleson followed Karl around the side of the house. Fortunately, the moon rode high in the sky, bathing the landscape in enough light to see Henrietta, her back up against a tree, and the three wraiths that surrounded her.

Karl shouted at them. One of the wraiths turned to face him. The others closed on Henrietta.

Mendleson raced along the uneven ground, holding his sword high. He hoped to get to Henrietta before they could hurt her. When he saw he couldn't, he shouted like Karl had, and another wraith turned to face him.

The wraith came at him swiftly, its arms held up. Mendleson brought the sword down on its head, knocking it sideways, but it was not enough to stop them from colliding. The sword hadn't killed it, either. The wraith clawed at him, tried to bring him to the ground.

Mendleson felt the claws tear his skin, just like the last one had. But this time, he had the sword. He pushed the thing off him, turned the sword in his hand, and swung. By luck or fate, he would never know, his blade severed the wraiths head from its body.

The body fell to to the ground and continued to twitch and writhe.

He looked at Henrietta and saw the third wraith had its hand on her forehead. Mendleson yelled, but it ignored him. It had what it wanted.

Mendleson ran toward it, sword extended, and ran it through the neck from the side. It fell away from Henrietta, and Henrietta slumped to the ground. Mendleson turned to the wraith, which was trying to get back up, and chopped at its neck until the head rolled away.

The night fell quiet. Mendleson looked for Karl and found him sprawled out on the ground, covered in blood. The wraith he had fought lay near him, twitching, but dead.

Mendleson dropped his sword and checked on

Henrietta. She was breathing, but her breaths were slow. She felt cold to his touch. A pack lay near her. She had been leaving.

Why?

But he knew why. She was trying to save him. *But if you were trying to save me, why call out? Why call for help?*

It didn't make any sense to him at the moment.

He picked her up and took her over to Karl.

When he got closer to Karl, he saw that Karl's wounds were worse than he thought. Karl lay gasping, his head turned to the side, his mouth leaking blood.

Mendleson set Henrietta down and went to Karl's side. "Karl?"

"I'm still here," Karl croaked. "They all dead?"

"They're dead."

"Henrietta?"

"I don't know. She's breathing."

Karl coughed, spitting out more blood. "You must take her to the Oracle."

"What? She told me that you wouldn't tell her how to find the Oracle."

"She didn't tell me..."

"Tell you what?"

"About you. Take her... Across the river. Find the path. It leads to a ravine. The ravine will lead you to the Oracle."

"What about you?"

"I'm dying."

"But she talked of a price..."

Karl hacked up even more blood, then spit it onto the ground. "There is always a price. I wasn't willing to pay. But you..."

"What price?"

A spasm ran through Karl's body, his eyes rolled back, and then a last bubble of blood escaped through his lips.

Mendleson looked around at the carnage, wondering what he should do about it, if anything, but he decided helping Henrietta was more important.

He picked her up again, said a silent prayer for Karl, and went back into the house to dress his wounds and clothe himself before trying to search out the Oracle.

He hoped he could find her in time.

SEVENTEEN

Inside the house, Mendleson laid Henrietta on his bed while he took time to bind his own wounds. They weren't nearly as severe as the ones he had received in his last battle with a wraith.

When he finished, he checked on her and saw that she was still breathing just as shallow as she had been outside.

He dressed, gathered their things and stuffed them into his pack, then scoured the house for things he might use. A rope, light cooking utensils, heavier clothing. The trip into the mountains was bound to grow colder the farther they traveled.

He took the pack out to the stable, stopping to pick up the sword that he had used against the wraiths. He saddled the horse, and then hung the pack from the saddle. He strapped the sword against it, too. When he was done readying the horse, he went back in for Henrietta.

He lifted her off the bed and carried her outside, then put her on the horse, leaning forward, her head off to the side so that she could breathe. The horse seemed curious as to what Mendleson was doing, turning its head to watch him.

"I should have asked about your name," he said. "Now you're all I've got to talk to."

He tied Henrietta down so that she would not fall, and then lead the horse out of the small stable and into the night.

"What do you think," he asked the horse. "Is there a bridge across this river? I really don't want to swim."

When they reached the river, Mendleson was disappointed. It wasn't much of a river. Only a few paces across at best. He'd also hoped for a bridge right behind Karl's home, but he didn't have that much luck. He found a stick and poked at the river bottom with it. The bottom fell away only a couple feet out, and the current tugged relentlessly at the stick.

"More deep than wide," he said. "Which way, do you think?" he asked the horse.

The horse looked at him, blinked in the moonlight, as if to ask why Mendleson didn't know the way himself.

"Fine. Upstream," he decided, thinking that at least they'd be heading into the mountains and closer to the Oracle, and that maybe, nearer the falls the town was named for, the river might grow shallow enough so that he could cross without swimming.

He assumed there had to be a crossing close by.

After a short time, he did find a foot bridge that

spanned the river, but he didn't think it would be strong enough for the horse. Below the bridge, the current ran swift between the banks.

He stared at the bridge for a while before deciding he'd have to carry Henrietta across himself. He'd have to hope the horse would swim across to him.

He took the pack off the horse first and strapped it to his back, then untied Henrietta and brought her down into his arms.

His first step onto the bridge told him he had been right about the bridge's ability to carry the horse. With each additional step, the wood creaked and groaned, and he worried that the next step might be the one that broke through and carried him into the river.

When he was about half way across, he heard a splash behind him. He spun around and saw that the horse had jumped in the river and was now swimming across.

"I wish I had something for you, horse," he said as his fear about not having a horse to carry Henrietta dissipated.

He continued on to the other side and said a silent prayer, thanking the Fates for not dropping him and Henrietta into the river.

Soon, he had Henrietta back on the now wet horse, and the three of them set off to find the trail that Karl had said would lead him to the Oracle.

‡

Mendleson found the trail with ease, even in the fading moonlight. Traveling it was a little more difficult with Henrietta on the horse. More times than he could count, he had to hack away with the sword at low hanging branches that prevented the horse and its unconscious burden from passing.

At one point, after hacking through a branch that was as big around as his arm, he turned to Henrietta and said, "I'm beginning to wonder if carrying you would be easier."

But he had no real idea how much farther he had to travel.

The trail began to climb, only making the going harder. It switched back on itself more than once, and sometimes thinned to the point that the horse barely fit through gaps between trees, or between a tree and a rock outcropping.

Mendleson checked on Henrietta often, hoping she might wake. But always, she continued her shallow breathing and her eyes did not flutter and open.

"Why did they come this time?" he asked her silent figure. "And why were you outside, looking like you were leaving?"

He led the horse around a large outcropping of stone. He worried that soon it would grow too difficult for the horse to walk.

"Did they come because you were leaving, Henrietta? Or did you decide to go somewhere else?

What hurts the most is that you left so soon after I thought we had finally understood each other.

"No," he said. "What hurts the most is that you're hurt."

He almost ran his head into a tree that had fallen across the trail. He could climb under, or over, but the trail had ended for the horse.

He wanted to yell, scream, and hurl invective at the Fates, but he kept his most angry thoughts to himself, asking only, "Why does this have to be so hard?"

No answer came to him.

He took everything off the horse, then brought Henrietta down and set her next to the fallen log. He went to the horse and patted it on the neck. "You've been good to us. I wish I didn't have to leave you here, but you can't go where we're going."

Mendleson slung his pack over his shoulder. He picked up the sword and slipped it between the pack and his back.

He squated down and squeezed himself under the tree, then reached back for Henrietta and pulled her under with him.

Henrietta was light enough that he could carry her and his pack, but he hoped the Oracle wasn't too much farther.

I wonder if I should rest before continuing on. He decided against it. He had no idea if Henrietta would wake on her own, or if she would need help, or could be helped. The thought that the Oracle might not be able to help almost brought tears to his eyes, but he fought them back.

This is not going to be like Mirrielle! This is not going to happen again!

Those thoughts pushed him forward and up a trail that grew more and more treacherous to his footing.

When the moon set, he wondered how long he had until the sun rose. They hadn't been traveling at night the last week. He had little sense of its journey anymore, and this close to the mountains, he had little idea when the sun might rise above them.

When he stumbled over a stone that he couldn't see and nearly dropped Henrietta, he decided it was time to rest until he had more than just starlight to guide him.

He felt around until he discovered a patch of ground that seemed less rocky, and set Henrietta down there. Once her weight was gone from him, the built up ache that he had been ignoring asserted itself as cramps in his arms. He spent a few minutes rubbing at them until he could get the pain to subside.

He sat down next to Henrietta, put his head near her mouth, and listened to her breathe.

"I hope morning light will reveal good news," he said, and then lay back himself and stared up at the stars.

‡

Mendleson didn't feel like opening his eyelids. The sun warmed them. Opening them meant he would have to move.

But resting wouldn't get Henrietta to the Oracle any sooner.

He rolled so that he faced Henrietta and opened his eyes. He couldn't tell if she was getting better or worse. Her chest still rose and fell slowly. Her skin was pale, but he hadn't seen it in good light the night before.

He turned over to reach into his pack and got his first good look at where he was. Stones and rocks littered the trail, making it almost more rock than dirt. Trees surrounded him and Henrietta, tall and thick with age. In the direction the trail would lead them, it looked like the trees were thinning out.

He reached into his pack, pulled out the remaining dried pork, and quickly ate it while wishing that he had more of Karl's stew to eat instead.

When he finished, he stood, strapped the pack to his back, and then bent down to pick up Henrietta. She seemed lighter than he remembered, but still substantial enough that he couldn't carry her forever. It wasn't quite like lugging bags of feed around, either.

"This hike had better not take much longer," he said, stepping out onto the trail to resume his journey.

After a mile, perhaps a little more, the trail led him to a small stream. The trail turned to follow the stream toward its source. He looked upstream, and saw that the trees thinned out even more.

His legs ached. He thought about setting Henrietta down and taking a rest. A look at her caused him to choose otherwise. Her breathing had slowed, and where she had been pale before, her skin now looked nearly translucent. It didn't take much on his part to deduce that she might die on him if he couldn't get her to the Oracle. He hoped the Oracle could even help. Seers weren't known for their healing powers.

He turned upstream and picked up his pace as much as he could on the uneven trail. It grew more and more difficult to traverse the farther he went. Larger stones, less soil. He had to keep his eyes on the trail right in front of him to find the best route.

His legs grew tired from the uneven footing. His arms and back grew sore from carrying Henrietta. The stream next to him bubbled along, not caring that he hurt.

A stone Mendleson stepped on slipped under him and rolled. A sharp pain ran through his ankle as it turned from exhaustion and the weight he carried. He fell to the ground, adjusting his fall so that Henrietta would land on him. She came down on his chest, driving the air from his lungs.

After several gasps, he got his wind back. "Why!" he shouted. His shout echoed back to him.

When he looked about, he found that he the ground had risen up around him while he concentrated on the path in front of him. He was in a ravine. *Is this it? Am I here?*

He hoped so.

He gently pushed Henrietta off of him, then reached down to his ankle to check it out. He prodded at it, but the prodding didn't produce any sharp pains. The ankle was just sore.

He got to his feet and tested it out a bit, walking around. He could put weight on it. It hurt, but he would live.

He bent down and picked up Henrietta. His ankle shrieked at the additional weight, but after a moment, it subsided enough to let him try a few steps.

The first step was the most painful. He grimaced and clenched his teeth. He couldn't put all of his and Henrietta's combined weight on it for very long. He had to adopt a hobbling gate that was sure to slow him down, and every step on that ankle caused his body to shake.

But he didn't give up, he didn't set her down. He'd committed to saving her, and he wouldn't let her down.

Step after painful step, he muddled his way through the ravine, hoping to find a cottage and an Oracle at the end of it.

EIGHTEEN

Mendleson fell to his knees, nearly dropping Henrietta. His body wouldn't let him go even one step farther. The ravine and the wraiths had defeated him. He had failed Henrietta. Another wraith would come, and this time, he could not stop it from taking what it wanted.

He laid Henrietta down in front of him and reached out to caress her face. Her cheeks were cold, even in the warmth of the mid-afternoon sun.

"I'm sorry I couldn't do more," he whispered.

He pulled the sword out in case the wraiths chose to come after them while he rested. "Of course, if they don't give me a chance to rest, I'll hardly be able to swing it.

"I just wish I knew where the damned Oracle was," he said. His voice echoed from the walls of the ravine.

When the echo died out, the only sound to answer was the bubbling of the stream. It soothed him, whispered him to sleep, whispered that everything would be all right.

But he knew it lied. It couldn't be all right. Henrietta was going to die here, next to him, and he would be able to do little, if anything, to stop it, unless the wraiths gave him time to rest.

He allowed himself to lay on the ground, holding the sword to his chest, and closed his eyes. He decided he should take whatever time he could. A few minutes, an hour, the rest of the afternoon. "The Oracle can't be much farther."

"You could not be more correct," said a woman's voice from above him.

Mendleson opened his eyes and tried to sit up, but the sword had suddenly grown heavy, and it held him down.

A figure stood over him, shrouded in a dark cloak. Its head blocked the late afternoon sun, leaving the face in darkness. He struggled against the sword, but it would not budge. "Go away!" he shouted, thinking the figure a wraith. "Leave her alone!"

The figure knelt, changing the angle of the light and allowing a ray of it to reflect off the face inside the hood. A woman, not a wraith. "I thought you were bringing her to me. Is this not so?"

Mendleson stopped struggling. Even with the bit of light that illuminated her face, he still couldn't get a good look at her. At times, the shadows made her seem about the age of Henrietta, but a slight shift of her head would cause her features to appear like they had seen many more winters than even Henrietta's uncle. "You're not a wraith," he said.

She laughed. "I should say not. They cannot enter my land."

"Then are you the Oracle?" he asked.

"Some call me so."

"Then you knew we were coming?"

"I am no Seer, young man. I did not know you were coming until you crossed the boundary."

"Can you help her?"

"It is within my ability," she said.

Mendleson thought it a strange answer. He turned his head a bit, hoping to get a better look at her, but her face continued to shift its appearance. "What do you mean?" he asked.

"I do not know if I should. Does she even desire help?"

"Of course she wants help," he said. He pushed at the sword again, but it still held him in place.

"There is no need to struggle," she said. "I will not hurt you."

"But you won't help her."

"Do not misconstrue my words young swordsman. I have not said that I will refuse help. I have only said that I am not sure if I should supply it. You struggle against the powers that rule this world. I must weigh what it will cost me if I interfere."

Mendleson gave up his struggle against the sword. "Please."

The woman smiled. "Much better. I will consider it. Put that hunk of iron away and come with me."

The extra weight of the sword melted away, and he found he could move. He stood slowly. Every muscle shouted at him to stop, but he ignored the shouts and forced himself up from the ground. He slipped the sword back between his pack and his body.

The woman had already started up the ravine.

"What about Henrietta?" he asked.

"Bring her," she said without turning around.

Silently, he cursed her. *You could help.*

She continued moving away from him, and he decided he'd better get on with it before he lost her. He bent down to pick up Henrietta, readying himself for the aches he knew he would feel.

But when he picked her up, she had lost all her weight. She encumbered him only as much as a large pillow might.

Witch. The word floated through his mind. Fear welled up within him.

He looked down at Henrietta's pale face. He blocked off that well of fear and refused to allow it to take over. The Oracle was Henrietta's only chance.

If she doesn't help, he thought as he took his first step to follow the woman, *I swear I will make her pay.*

‡

Mendleson carried the unnaturally light Henrietta inside the small, round, stone hut the witch called home. A bit of light streamed in through openings in the walls that he hesitated to call windows. It showed him only a single room, a fire pit in the center, a pallet against the wall for sleeping, and a table and two chairs hugging the opposite wall. Where the walls did not host pallet or table, shelves adorned them, and the shelves held jars and pots and tools that Mendleson could not name.

The witch pointed to the pallet. "Set her there." Then she went to the wall and started searching through her jars.

Mendleson crossed the room with Henrietta, and then bent down and laid her gently on the bedding, which proved softer than it looked. He brushed away a lock of hair that had fallen across her face. He wanted to bend down and kiss her, touch his lips to hers.

How could this have happened?

He whispered to her. "Why did you try to leave last night? After..."

"After what?" the witch asked.

Mendleson turned to find her standing over him. "It's not important," he said.

"How can you know whether it's important? What did you do to her that made her leave?"

Mendleson stood up and faced her. She had removed the hood, and for the first time, he saw her face clearly. Her skin was youthful, like he had thought, but her eyes shone ancient and black. Her head bore a tattoo of a tree instead of hair. A branch of that tree trailed down the side of her head and onto her ear where it circled the lobe. She wore an ornament on that lobe that appeared to be an obsidian raven, creating the illusion that a raven was sitting on the branch.

"Thank you," she said, and then pushed him aside and bent down to minister to Henrietta.

"Why didn't you just ask me to move?" he asked.

The witch ignored him. She dipped her fingers in a jar of something that looked a lot like mud to Mendleson, and then spread that mud on Henrietta's face, her forehead, her eyelids, so that none of her skin remained visible.

"How does that..." he began.

"Quiet," she said, waving her mud covered hand behind her.

Mendleson decided he didn't need to know right at that moment. If the witch was going to help Henrietta, he'd do whatever she asked of him.

From behind her, he could see more of the tree tattoo. It had several branches, all bare of leaves, and the trunk ran down her neck. It reminded him of something he'd heard in a half-remembered child's tale, but he couldn't place it. He wondered if his exhaustion was playing tricks on his mind.

He moved across the room and pulled out one of the chairs from the table. The legs scraped loudly across the stone floor, and he looked up to see if the witch had reacted. If she had, he couldn't tell. Her hands were moving slowly over Henrietta's body, as if they were searching for something.

He let himself settle onto the chair, keeping an eye on the witch.

For all he could tell, she didn't seem like she had any intentions of hurting them, but Mendleson had never heard anything good about witches, and Karl's reluctance to send them to her only served to reinforce his wariness.

The witch began chanting in a low, deep voice that did not seem to match her speaking voice. It was slow, somber, and soothing. Mendleson felt his eyelids drooping.

He pushed off sleep as long as he could, but in the end, his exhaustion got the better of him and drew him down into an uncomfortable, fitful slumber.

✝

At first, Henrietta wandered alone in a fog that hung thick and cold in the air. It clung to her skin like cobwebs. It reminded her of a dream she'd had, but could not place.

The ground was flat, almost barren. In hours of wandering, she had not come across a single landmark that she could use to mark her progress in her journey. The light hadn't changed, either. She expected it should be near dusk, with the number of hours she had traveled, but the light was as even, filtered, and gray as when she first found herself in this place.

Something troubled her about that. She couldn't remember arriving, or even where she had been just before. She felt something had happened, that she'd lost something, or nearly lost something, or someone. But her memory was just as hazy and empty as the foggy land she found herself in.

She probed at the haze, but nothing came to the fore. She needed a reminder, and she had nothing.

She continued to walk, in the hope that she would eventually find her way out of the fog. She resolved to keep walking until her legs gave out, until she needed to sleep, but after hours of wandering, she still wasn't tired.

She put step after step behind her. While she walked, she tried to think of what brought her to this place, and could come up with nothing but shadows.

"Why did they come this time?" A voice intruded into the silence, one she thought sounded familiar. "And why were you outside, looking like you were leaving?"

She spun around, and couldn't see anyone within her sight, just the gray fog in all directions. "Where are you?"

"Did they come because you were leaving, Henrietta?" the disembodied voice asked. "Or did you decide to go somewhere else? What hurts the most is that you left so soon after I thought we had finally understood each other."

"Who are you?" she asked. "What do you mean?"

"No," the voice said, as if it hadn't heard her. "What hurts the most is that you're hurt."

"I'm not hurt!" she shouted. "Where are you?"

The voice did not answer her.

"Hello?" she asked. "Who are you?"

She waited, but did not receive any answers. The voice was gone, wherever it had come from, leaving her confused. *Who are 'they'? Who was speaking, and why did he think she was hurt?*

She felt fear start to worm its way into her chest. "What's happening to me? Where am I?" She hoped the voice might answer her, but after her voice faded, no other sounds broke the silence she had previously been used to.

After several minutes passed with no change, she decided to press on through the fog and hope she could come to an end of it. The crunch of her footsteps on the loose ground comforted her.

She wondered for quite a while where the voice might have come from, and if it would come again. She kept listening for it. She somehow trusted that voice. But when she had traveled for several more hours and had not heard the voice again, she began to think she had imagined it.

Just when she had convinced herself that she had imagined it, she heard the voice again, only this time in a whisper. "I'm sorry I couldn't do more."

Her heart skipped. She whirled around again, looking for the speaker. He seemed so close to her, but she saw nothing. "Where are you? Please, show yourself!"

Again, she waited, calling out every couple of minutes, hoping the owner of the voice would show himself. But the fog remained unbroken, and she remained alone. The more she thought about it, the voice had sounded sad.

"Just tell me where you are," she said. "I can help you!"

She could only hear the beating of her heart. The voice was gone again.

She resumed walking.

Step after step, she walked toward the unchanging horizon that extended only a few yards around her.

Until a barren tree, its branches twisting through the mist, appeared in front of her. *A leafless oak tree,* she thought. *Leafless and lifeless.*

But it brought her hope. The creeping fear that she was wandering in circles subsided. A different unease filtered through her. Something about the tree made her wary.

She approached it slowly, eyes exploring it, looking for any sign of life, any sign of danger.

As she stepped in under the canopy of branches, the fog cleared away, its cobweb touch no longer fouling her. A raven squawked, and she looked up to see it standing on a branch near the trunk, looking down at her with beady black eyes.

"Who are you?" she asked it, but it only stared at her, apparently deeming its one warning squawk sufficient.

Choosing to ignore the raven for the moment, Henrietta looked about her and the tree, hoping to find evidence that this tree would lead her to others. But the tree appeared to live on an island in the fog. She could see no other trees beyond it.

From behind her, she thought she heard a woman singing softly. She spun around to meet this woman, but found only the tree and the raven. The song still sounded like it was coming from behind her. She spun again to find nothing but the fog.

"Show yourself," she said. "I can hear your singing."

The song continued, unbroken. It soothed her, and something else happened. She felt herself growing weary. Her legs ached with the effort from walking.

She thought it odd that only a minute earlier, she had felt no sign of fatigue.

"Who are you? The song is beautiful." Henrietta waited again, but still did not receive an answer.

She turned to face the tree again. The trunk looked like a good place to rest. She went to it, set her back against the trunk, and settled to the ground.

Come back, Henrietta. She thought the words were in the song, but when she listened closer, she heard only a wordless song.

She looked up to the raven. Her eyelids had grown heavy from the moment she sat. She thought they tricked her. A woman sat on the branch the raven had previously occupied. She was bald, but for a tattoo.

She blinked, and saw the raven sitting there again.

Close your eyes.

Find your way.

More words. They reached out to her, called to her.

She fought to keep her eyes open and focused on the raven. She wanted to see if it would change again. She thought she should recognize the woman, but recognition evaded her.

The sky grew dark.

She could no longer keep her eyes open. She thought she saw the raven smile as she let them close.

Who are you that sings? Henrietta asked in thought. She could not make the words come out.

But it didn't matter that the voice didn't answer. Her mind emptied, and the wordless song pulled her down into a dreamless sleep.

NINETEEN

"She sleeps," said the witch.

Mendleson lifted his head from the table where he had been sleeping. "Is she all right?" He looked to where Henrietta rested across the room. He started to get up to go to her.

"Sit, do not go to her," said the woman, motioning for him to stay seated. "She is out of danger, for now."

A wave of relief swept through him, until the last part of her statement reached his ears. "What do you mean?"

"Only that she will wake, and she will be fine, until the wraiths come for her."

"I don't understand. You said they wouldn't come here."

"And they won't, not while I am here. But I cannot stay here forever, and neither can the two of you."

Mendleson had no desire to stay near this woman. "I had only thought of staying long enough to see her well and to ask for your help."

"I have given help, have I not?"

"You have, and I am thankful. But that was not the help for which we sought you."

The witch turned her head a little, and the obsidian raven in her ear sparkled in a stray shaft of light. "Then why did you seek me?"

"We hoped you might tell us how she could avoid her fate."

The woman's eyes narrowed. "Avoid her fate? That is not something easily done."

"But she'll die," Mendleson said.

"We all die. Now, later. Death is not something one can avoid."

"But she's still young. Isn't there something we can do?"

The witch stood and went to the fire pit. Mendleson noticed for the first time that it was lit, and a pot hung over it. It smelled like a spicy vegetable soup.

The woman bent down to it, grabbed a bowl from a pile of them that lay nearby, and ladled soup into it until it was full.

"Aren't you going to answer me?" Mendleson asked, indignant at being ignored.

"It is not something that can be answered until I have talked to her." She came back to the table and set the bowl in front of Mendleson.

Mendleson stared at her. "But you can help?"

"Eat up," she said and wandered back across the room.

"Please," he said. "Tell me you can help."

The witch turned around and looked at him, her eyes gold in the light of the fire. "What makes you think you need help? You young people fight and fight and fight your fate. You do not seek to understand it. You do not think to ask why. Eat your soup."

She turned away from him, ending the conversation.

He sniffed at the soup and his stomach rumbled. "I'll try to understand, if you'll help me," he said before he stuck a spoonful of soup into his mouth.

It felt warm and soothing to his tongue, and it had just enough pepper to bring it to life. He swallowed and let it slide down his throat to his empty stomach. The tension in him left as the soup found its destination. Quickly, he spooned more of it into his mouth. Before he knew it, the bowl was empty.

He glanced at Henrietta. The witch hadn't yet removed the mud from Henrietta's face, and it gave her a look similar to the primitives he'd seen on the slave ships that occasionally stopped for supplies back home. They never stayed long. He'd wondered where they came from, and where they were being taken, but he had never had the opportunity to find out. He didn't think anyone in town had ever asked.

"When will she wake?" Mendleson asked.

The witch was sitting by the fire, knitting something from a dark red yarn. It was too small, yet, to get a sense of its ultimate shape. "Soon, I should think," she said without looking up from her work.

"Thanks for the soup," he said. "It was delicious."

"You're welcome. It seems to have helped your mood, too."

It had. Mendleson felt much more content with the situation. The witch would tell him what he needed to know once Henrietta awakened.

"Tell me of your wife," said the witch.

"My wife," he said, reflecting back. "She was beautiful. Auburn hair, a freckle to the right of her right eye. She was everything to me. We'd known each other from childhood. Her mother died when she was young, and for a long time, her father tried to keep us apart." Curiously, Mendleson did not feel sad as he thought back to that time.

"He didn't succeed," she said.

"No. Well, he did succeed, until he too passed away just about the time Mirrielle came of age. I asked my parents to take her in, but they would have nothing of it. They said they could barely feed us. I didn't realize until later that was the reason behind her father's attempts to keep us apart. He wanted her to marry into a wealthy family."

The witch grunted, but said nothing.

"So I went to Mirrielle with a plan, and we ran away down the coast to where I learned to be a fisherman. It wasn't easy at first, but I seemed to have a gift for it. Eventually, I was able to purchase my own boat, and then my own land."

The witch looked up. "You're telling me about you. I want to hear about her."

Mendleson nodded, wondering what exactly the witch wanted to hear.

"She cared for our land, a small farm, while I was out fishing. I didn't see her as much as I would have liked. Especially later."

"Was she happy?"

Mendleson thought back to the times he would see Mirrielle. She always had a smile on her face when she saw him. But when it was time for him to go to sea, she sometimes urged him to stay, to help her on the farm. "She seemed happy. We loved each other."

"She didn't want you to go fishing."

Mendleson shook his head. "Sometimes she begged me to stay."

"Why wouldn't you stay?"

"The sea called to me. I made a good living from it."

"Yet you gave it up when she died."

Mendleson stood up, knocking against the small table. "How did you know that?"

The witch kept knitting. His outburst did not even cause her to flinch. "It is my business to know."

"How is it a witch's business to know something about me that I haven't told you? And if you know that, then you know what she was like and you don't even have to ask me."

She slowly turned her head to face him, and she set

her hands in her lap. "First, Mendleson, I am no more a witch than you. Witches deal in nature and how nature can be used to corrupt or cure the ailings and failings of men. I am altogether different."

"What are you?"

"She is one of the Fates," said Henrietta. Her voice was week, but she was sitting up. "Lindyral, I think."

"Hen," Mendleson said, forgetting the conversation. He ran to her and knelt beside her. "How do you feel?"

"I ache, I'm hungry, and my face itches."

‡

Henrietta suffered the cold damp cloth without complaining. The woman, the Fate, had put mud on her face which had dried and caused it to itch. Henrietta didn't complain because she was alive, and Mendleson was with her.

While Lindyral ministered to her, Mendleson filled her in on how she had come to be cared for by a Fate.

A Fate. Henrietta had never thought to meet one. They were beings of myth, hidden pullers of strings, legends in stories handed down from one Seer to another. It had to be more than coincidence that the only one she had ever cared to learn about was Lindyral, who was said to be the caretaker of the Seer's Gift. She had never learned that Lindyral was any more accessible than the rest of the fates.

When Mendleson told her of her uncle's death, sadness superseded her wonder at finding Lindyral. She remembered the times she had spent with him after her mother had died, after his wife had died. They hadn't been completely happy times, but they had been better than the alternative.

And he had been the only man in her life since that time, or even before that time. She couldn't even remember her father.

She had guilt, too, that she was responsible for his death. If she hadn't come this way, if she hadn't involved him in her troubles, he would be alive right now.

She had to close her eyes. She could feel tears trying to come, and she didn't want them. She didn't want Mendleson to notice.

He noticed anyway. "Are you alright?" he asked, interrupting his story.

She shook her head. Lindyral pulled away from her.

"Don't blame yourself, Henrietta," he said.

She opened her eyes, and saw him looking at her. *How does he know that I'm blaming myself?* "I'm not," she said.

He put his hand out and ran it through her hair. His strong fingers on her scalp soothed her. She wanted him to pull her close. "Good," he said, "because you've been telling me the same thing for weeks. You didn't make his decision to come to your rescue for him."

"But I didn't have to bring them here," she said,

unable to keep her thoughts from escaping. "I could have gone somewhere else."

Lindyral dabbed at her face with the cloth again. "Don't be so sure that you could have done anything else, young Seer. You have long sought to avoid your fate, yet you are still here."

Henrietta pushed the woman's hand from her face. "What would you know about it?" she asked. But she knew as soon as she said it how foolish the question was. Of course Lindyral would know what she had done. Seers were her responsibility.

Fortunately, Lindyral didn't answer her directly. "Be assured, Henrietta, that your uncle had his chances to avoid his fate, and he made his choices."

Henrietta hated having to be told that. If what Mendleson said were true, Mendleson and her uncle did not have to risk their lives at all. They could have let the wraiths take her sight and her life. Mendleson could have saved himself by doing nothing.

She examined him, the gray-green flecks in his eyes, the sun-browned skin that was now covered in dirt, the slightly flared nostrils, the way the corners of his mouth now seemed to want to turn up where they used to lean down.

"Mendleson hasn't had choices to make," she said.

"He hasn't? He's been making choices since he met you, dear. You're so wrapped up in your need to suffer alone that you can't see that others want to help you."

"But I'm going to die in the next few days!"

"Are you so sure? Can you see past the loss of your sight?"

"Of course I can't see beyond it, but I have never heard of any Seer surviving the loss." *Could it be possible? No. It can't be. My mother, my aunt, my grandmother, they all died.*

"And because you have never heard of it means it can't happen, so you gave up on your life and never let anyone get close to you."

And now, she felt tears on her face. "I didn't want anyone to feel like I felt after my mother died."

"Don't cry, dear," said Lindyral. "It's admirable to want to spare others the pain you felt. But what was the price of your desire? How would your life have been different if you had made different choices?"

Henrietta wondered what would have happened if she'd never left her home, never stayed in Berelost, never went to the edge of the sea. Would her fate have changed? Would Mendleson's life be in danger now?

"I tried to make different choices," she said, "and it didn't get me anywhere." Her hands were trembling. She put them to her knees in an effort to still them, but it didn't help much. She looked to Mendleson and sought out his eyes. "All my efforts at making choices only served to drag Mendleson into my fate."

"Would you trade what you have known with him for the knowledge that he would be safe from sharing your fate?"

Henrietta looked deep into her heart, and it didn't take her long to know that she would not trade those moments, the shared closeness that had developed between them. They were a part of her now, and she couldn't imagine giving them up. "Yes," she lied, knowing she wouldn't ever have to make that trade.

Mendleson's eyes narrowed, unhappy with her response.

"Look at him, Henrietta," said the Fate. "Could you really trade the moments in the barn, the night you shared, knowing that he would have had a different fate, knowing that he might now be dead had he not gone with you?"

"What?" she and Mendleson asked at the same time. They had both turned to face the Fate.

She smiled, causing the raven in her ear to shift. "Only speculation on my part. I am no Seer. But you are so sure that the fate he now shares with you is worse than the one he would have had if you had never met."

"But..."

"No, do not question me on this. You can only see the branch of the tree as it stands. It is all the power a Seer has. Once a different branch has passed, it is unknowable. If you had never met with him at the festival, he might still have been home when the storm that overtook you at Berelost knocked his home to the ground and nearly washed the whole town from the coast."

Mendleson gasped, and Henrietta felt shivers run through her limbs. "It's gone?" he asked.

The Fate nodded. Mendleson's skin went white. "My friends..."

"I would not tell you, even if I could," she said. "I should not have said as much as I have. I will pay for that."

Henrietta's heart went out to him. She knew he had friends there, and he'd left them for her.

And now, her mind rebelled at the possibilities. If she had left him there, he might have died, but he might have lived and might have helped his friends. But she had taken him from that fate, just by following a vision she had been given.

"Who gave me the vision?" she asked. "Which one of you are responsible?"

"Vision?"

"Don't play coy," she said, standing up. "The vision that led me to meet Mendleson at the festival. Who gave it to me? Was it you?"

"I do not give visions, child. You know that."

"I only know the stories. If it wasn't you, then who was it?"

"Why does it matter? Your meeting likely saved his life."

"You don't know that." Henrietta was truly angry. "He might have saved other lives. He might have helped his friends. Whoever sent me that vision robbed him of that possibility."

Lindyral shook her head. "He still had choices, dear. He could have chosen differently."

Henrietta stamped her foot on the packed earth floor with a less than satisfying thud. "Did he really have a choice?" she asked, then she turned and left the one room hut. She couldn't handle being near that woman any longer.

‡

Mendleson watched Henrietta's exit in a state of shock. He knew he should go after her, keep her from wandering too far, but he had his own questions for Lindyral.

"Were you telling the truth, or just making a point? Would I have died?" he asked her. His legs wanted him to stand up, to follow Henrietta, but he refused to give into them.

"Like I told the Seer, once a branch has been followed, there is no way to know for sure what would have happened had the other paths been followed instead. Could you have died? Yes. Would you have? There is no way for me to know."

"What about my friends?"

The Fate chuckled. "You are not my charge, and I am no messenger. I do not know the fates of your friends."

"But..."

"No," she said, standing and turning to confront him, all traces of chuckle gone. "I am not all-powerful. I am a single Fate, not all of them. My charge is to see that the Gift is passed on from Seer to Seer. What happens to you is none of my concern.

"If you wish to see her live beyond the taking, you should go to her."

Mendleson turned to go, frustrated that she wouldn't answer him. He seethed inside. He wanted to rush home to help his friends, to find out whether they even lived, but his need for Henrietta had grown, and his desire for her to live pulled at him with equal strength.

Something else bothered him, and he turned back to face Lindyral. "But aren't you the Oracle of Arabeth?"

The flames in the fire-pit flickered as a great rush of wind entered the hut, causing strange shadows from the Fate to flash across the walls. She rose up, almost floating, and for the first time, she did not seem even remotely human. "Leave this place!"

Mendleson stumbled backward, fell through the door and out of the hut, to land on his back amongst the stones that littered the ground. His heart pounded in his chest, and his limbs trembled. He looked up to the stars and took a few deep breaths while he pondered what had just happened.

He couldn't make any sense of it at all. He hadn't thought much about what might happen when he left to follow Henrietta, but he never imagined that he wouldn't be able to go back to his home, to his friends, after it was over.

It hurt, but not nearly as much as he thought it

should. And even though Henrietta had said he could be there helping people, when he thought about it, he didn't feel like that's what he should be doing.

No. I should be with Henrietta. That's what feels right. I just wish I knew how to help her, and that Fate, the Oracle, doesn't seem like she's interested in helping at all. In fact, he thought, *it seems our being here might be just as much her doing as anything else.*

Which frightened him. He knew why he tried to help Henrietta initially, and he thought he knew why he hadn't given up trying to help. *But now, I can't even trust that my feelings for her are my own.*

TWENTY

Henrietta walked down to the edge of the stream and found a rock to sit on. She stayed in sight of the cottage. She worried a bit about the wraiths, wondering if they would come for her here, but felt that she was safe for the moment.

She looked up at the sky and found it clear. The stars shone as bright as she could remember having seen them, and they were a comfort to her. There was possibility in them, and certainty. They hung in the sky, every night, always in the same pattern as they moved through their slow progression.

She remembered back to a time when she had listened to her grandmother tell her that the stars were the eyes of the Fates looking down on them. Henrietta had wondered which one was her fate. The memory grew hazy. She couldn't remember exactly what her grandmother had said. Just an admonishment against looking to the stars for her fate.

But since then, Henrietta had always wondered, when she looked up, which was hers.

Having met Lindyral, though, she no longer thought the stars were fates. The stars were too constant and distant for that to be possible. She couldn't imagine one of them interfering in her life, or interfering in Mendleson's.

It has to be that woman, she thought. *What I can't figure out is why. Why is it so important that I lose my sight here in the mountains? Why do I have to come here to die?*

Behind her, the dim light escaping the cottage flared up, causing her to turn just as Mendleson fell backward through the door.

Why did that woman have to make me responsible for his death, and why does she now have the stones to tell me that it might have saved his life?

Mendleson didn't get up right away, and a tingle of fear ran through her. *What happened?*

She stood and shouted out to him. "Mendleson!"

He rolled on to his side, and she breathed a sigh of relief. He pushed himself up to his feet, and when he started walking her way, she sat back down on the rock and waited for him.

When he was near enough she didn't have to shout, she asked, "What happened?"

She could only see an outline of his face in the starlight as he shook his head. "I don't know," he said.

"I asked her a question, and she got angry with me. The fire flared up, and for a moment, she no longer looked human."

"What did she look like?" she asked.

"I don't know. I can't describe it."

He made as if he wanted to sit down next to her. She moved to make room for him. When his body pushed up against hers, she felt a different tingle than the tingle of fear.

"What did you ask her that made her so upset?" She let her hand fall so that it touched his thigh.

"The last thing I asked was if she was the Oracle of Arabeth, but I don't think that was the only thing that made her upset."

"What do you think it was, then?"

"I kept pushing to find out about my friends back home," he said. "She wouldn't answer me. She said she wasn't my fate."

She could feel his warmth, and she snuggled in closer to him. The air around them felt chilly. "Did she say anything else?"

"She told me I had to come for you if I wished to see you live beyond the taking. I didn't understand that at all."

Henrietta's breath caught in her throat. *I can live!*

Then she thought about what that might mean, about what her vision meant for Mendleson. "Leave me now, Mendleson. Save yourself. I may get to live, but I'm sure that you'll die."

He turned to face her, and even though they were shadowed, she thought she could see his dark green eyes as they took her in. "If she's right, I have no place to go. My home is in ruins."

"That doesn't mean you have to die for me. Everyone I've ever loved has died. My mother, my aunt, my grandmother, and now my uncle. And every one of them died trying to protect me." She reached up and touched his stubbled cheek, let her hand slide around behind his neck. "I don't want that fate for you, too."

"What about what I want?" he asked. She could feel his breath on her lips. "I don't want you to die. I realize now that my wife's death was not my fault, and I've accepted it, but if you think for a moment that I wouldn't do everything within my power to save your life, you're a fool."

She didn't know why, but his assertion made her feel warm inside, not angry. "A fool?" *Am I really a fool?*

"Yes. If you push me away, you're a fool. Let me in. Let me help you."

Henrietta just couldn't imagine doing that. She pulled her hand from his neck and leaned away. "I can't, Mendleson. I can't see you hurt."

"Then, please, come inside and talk to that woman. She thinks you can live beyond the loss of your sight. At least listen to her for me. What harm could that do?"

"Only if you promise me one thing."

"What?"

"Promise me that once I've heard what she has to say, you'll leave."

"No," he whispered.

"Promise me, Mendleson. Promise me you'll go live another life, or I won't go listen to her."

He stood up and backed away from her. "I can't do it," he said. She could hear the anguish in his voice. She hated it.

But she couldn't let him die for her. She stood, too. "If you don't promise me, I will walk out into those woods and let the wraiths take me." *Mother! Grandmother! What do I do? I'm hurting him, but I can't let him die for me!*

After tortured moments, he bowed his head. "I promise," he said, and then he turned back to the cottage and left her standing at the edge of the stream.

She ran after him with a thought toward holding him and telling him that it would all work out, but when she caught up to him, he resisted her touch.

Her heart ached, as she knew instinctively that she had managed to create a barrier between them that hadn't been there before. Somehow, she had thought she'd feel better about convincing him to leave, but instead there was now an emptiness in her heart that she hadn't known had been filled.

They walked back to the cottage together in silence, and just about as far apart as they'd been since their meeting at the festival.

‡

Back in the Fate's hut once again, Mendleson tried to stay as far away from the woman as possible. He was grateful that the Fate took Henrietta across the room so that the two of them could talk together without being overheard.

He kept telling himself, as he sat at the table watching them, that he should leave now, but he couldn't make himself do it. He'd given up far too much already to leave before he was sure Henrietta had listened to the woman and would do what was necessary to survive.

And as he watched them talk, he dreamed about her, thinking that maybe a day would come when he could be with her, thinking that he could find her again after he left.

She completely befuddled him. He'd thought she had accepted he would be there until the end after what had happened in the barn, and then at her uncle's home. He thought, when she woke, she would be grateful, that she would finally see what he'd come to see.

But she hadn't. She maneuvered him into a corner so that he had to give in to her demands.

And that had angered him. She was so stubborn, and for a woman given such an incredible gift of sight, she was blind. Blind to his need, and to her own.

They'd been weeks on the road together, and still she kept working to make him leave despite her obvious desire for him to stay.

She is the same as me. She can't accept that she's not responsible for the fate of others. He chuckled darkly to himself, and Henrietta turned her head to look at him, before turning back to the Fate. Her Fate.

Mendleson stood, then. *I've done all I can. It's time for me to go.*

With one last look at Henrietta, who didn't turn away from her conversation, he stepped out of the hut into the dark of the night, unsure of where he would go next.

‡

"You can't change the future through your actions," Lindyral said. "If you want a different future, my daughter, you must change your heart."

"I don't understand," said Henrietta. "How can changing my heart affect the future more than changing actions?"

"Every action that you take ultimately flows from your heart. In the short term, you can take an action that goes against your heart's desires, but your heart will ultimately undermine that action and your fate will not change."

Henrietta heard Mendleson chuckle from behind her, and she turned momentarily to look at him. He didn't seem to be chuckling at her. The look on his face was dark. She ached to walk over to him, to tell him he didn't have to leave. *But this is for his own good, isn't it?*

She turned back to Lindyral so that she wouldn't waver in her decision.

"But what about my heart must change? How do I avoid my Fate?"

"You cannot avoid me, my daughter. I must take your sight and pass it on to another."

"But Mendleson said you knew how I could live beyond that."

Henrietta heard a chair scrape, but didn't turn around. She didn't want to look at him again. Then she heard his footsteps, and knew he went outside. She knew he left.

She wanted to jump up, tell him not to go, to come back, that she was wrong. But she wasn't. It was better for him this way.

"That," said Lindyral, "is unfortunate."

"What? What do you mean?"

"Your love for him, and his for you, that was the easiest path to what you seek. I had hopes that you could change your heart, that you could learn to love and receive the sacrifice of others, and that you could do so without blaming yourself.

"Your aunt died because your uncle would not sacrifice of himself for her. Your mother blamed herself for your aunt's death. And you, you blame yourself for it all. Your heart is closed to real help from others."

"But I can't let him die for me!"

"It is of no matter, anymore," said Lindyral, with a look of concern and sadness on her face. "He is gone."

"No," Henrietta said.

She jumped up and ran to the door. She went outside into the night air and yelled at the top of her voice. "Mendleson!" Again and again, her voice echoed into the dark. He had to have heard her, but he didn't return.

For the first time since her mother died, she felt a real sense of loss, a hole in her heart, an emptiness where something had grown these past few weeks. Tears stung her eyes as she continued to cry out for him. "I'm sorry," she said.

She felt a hand on her shoulder, and after several more cries, she acknowledged the hand. "What have I done?"

"What you have always done," said Lindyral. "Come inside, and I will tell you of another possible way, but the result may not be what you want."

Henrietta followed her inside, a little bit of hope amidst her misery. "How is it different?"

"You would become a Fate."

TWENTY-ONE

Henrietta woke with the early morning sun streaming through the hole in the roof, bathing her face in its light. She'd hoped she'd dream again, that her vision of her end would have shown itself to her again, and that it would have changed.

But her night had been devoid of dreams, and she didn't know if Mendleson's leaving changed anything.

She stood up and stretched. Lindyral hadn't given her much more than a thin mat to sleep on. It was better than the ground, with which she was all too familiar lately, but it still left her shoulders and her back sore.

She looked around for Lindyral, and couldn't find her anywhere. She saw a plate on the table, and it held a loaf of bread and a vine of berries. She sat down to eat.

Putting berry after berry into her mouth, all she could do was think about Mendleson. After her conversation with Lindyral, she found herself wishing she hadn't driven him off. Her heart still ached because of it. More than once as she ate, she caught herself crying.

She choked the tears back each time. "Dammit Henrietta," she told herself after the third time. "You are not going to spend the day crying over your decision."

She finished the bread, and then stood up. She looked to the hearth. The coals were cold. Lindyral had seen to that before she stepped out.

No. It was obvious Lindyral was not coming back.

"I guess I got what I wanted," Henrietta said. *It's not what I wanted. It's what I asked for.*

She didn't have a pack, but where she was going, she didn't need one. "Less than a day's walk," Lindyral had said. "Up the trail until it ends."

What surprised Henrietta at first was that it was the same place her vision had her going. It seemed she hadn't changed her fate at all. *Perhaps,* she thought, *this is what it would have been all along had I not met Mendleson.*

The tears came again, and she wiped at her eyes. *I can't think about him. Think about the other possibility.*

To become a Fate. To be able to touch the world in a more direct way, to help people, the idea excited her.

She stepped out into the early-morning mountain sun and moved toward the trail at the top of the meadow that sat behind the hut. It was only near the stream where the ground was rocky. Elsewhere around the hut, the ground was covered in grasses that came to her thighs.

She thought about what Lindyral had told her while she waded through the grass.

"Becoming a Fate isn't the easy decision that it sounds like. You don't get to chose the lives you touch. You don't get to have contact with them unless they seek you out, and you will rarely, if ever, talk to another Fate. You will be alone—like the rest of us."

"That doesn't sound as bad as death," Henrietta had said.

"It doesn't? To never be able to talk to your love? To always remember the chance at love that you had and didn't take? I know what's been in your heart, and I am not sure that you would cherish becoming a Fate."

"Then why tell me about it?"

"So that you can make a choice. You came to me for advice, and it is my charge to provide it. I cannot tell you what to choose."

"I have time to choose?"

"If you are at the Standing Stone as the sun drops below the horizon, you will be given a choice. Think hard before then, for whatever choice you make, it cannot be undone."

Henrietta had asked more questions, until Lindyral told her that she would not answer another.

And now she was entering the forest on her way to the stone that she'd seen in her dreams all her life, and she found herself wishing Mendleson was with her. This time, the tears came, and she let them. There was no one to see.

✝

Henrietta emerged from the forest and onto the plateau, and she still hadn't made her decision. Her tears were gone for the moment, and she was happy for that. It let her look out over the edge of the plateau to see the world below, and the view took her breath for a time.

Because the sky was clear, she could see Berelost in the far, far distance. Closer, she could see the rivers and the lakes surrounded with trees. She saw farmland and roads. She felt almost like she could see the whole of the world.

She could also see the sun as it neared the horizon, a blazing orange ball that would herald her new life, or her death. It wouldn't be long, either. She had, at most, half an hour before the sun touched the horizon and began to sink out of sight.

She turned around, and for the first time with her own eyes, she saw the Standing Stone, the monolith, that she had envisioned since she was a girl.

It was hexagonal in shape. Its rounded top towered above her, some fifteen feet or more in height. Glyphs covered each of its black granite faces, glyphs she did not know how to read. It had been imposing in her dreams. Here, in front of her, it inspired a sense of awe. Her mind could not have brought words forth to describe the sense of ancient power that it radiated. There had been none of that in her vision.

What had Lindyral said? 'You only need embrace it, and say the words.'

But in its presence, she could not remember the words. Even having seen it, she wasn't sure she wanted to say them, anyway.

She thought she heard something in the trees, the snap of a branch, and she turned to look in that direction, but among the late evening shadows that inhabited the forest, she could see nothing that moved.

She turned around to watch the sun, to wait for it to complete its daily journey across the sky, to wait for her doom, whichever doom she chose. She knew it would happen tonight.

Fear crept through her. No matter what happened, she would lose what she was, she would lose her sight, and she would no longer be able to look forward along the branches of a life. If she chose to become a Fate, she would live for generations, but she would forever be denied another chance at a real life.

"If only I hadn't driven Mendleson away," she said softly. "I would have liked to say goodbye."

And, she realized, she would always be haunted by that mistake.

The bottom of the sun touched the world, and she knew the time had come at last. She would have to chose, and she didn't like either choice.

TWENTY-TWO

In the dark of the night, despite the light of the stars and the moon, Mendleson decided he wouldn't stray far from the hut. As angry as he was at Henrietta, the thought of leaving her still tore him apart, and he just couldn't make himself give up.

He reached the trees on the other side of the stream and then sat down just inside the tree line, leaving himself with a view of the hut.

When she came out, calling for him, he almost went to her. He could hear the anguish in her voice, and his body stood, and even took a step, but he wrestled control of his body away from his emotions.

She wanted this, he thought to himself. *She wanted me gone, and now I am.*

And when she finally gave up and went back inside, he let himself slide down against a tree, where he spent long hours pondering his decision before sleep stole over him.

Sunlight woke him as it broke over the top of the mountains. He was damp from early morning dew. There was a chill to the air, brought by a light breeze, but the sky was cloudless, and he knew the day would soon warm him.

He cast one last look at the hut before turning to head downstream.

He walked perhaps twelve feet before a short, older woman stepped out from behind a tree. He stumbled to the ground in his effort to avoid running her over.

"Careful," she said. "You don't want to hurt yourself."

She put out a hand to help him up, and he took it.

As soon as he had a good look at the woman, he let her hand drop, and he backed away.

Her head was shaved, covered in a tattoo of a tree, much like Lindyral, but this wasn't Lindyral. This was another Fate. She had a bird for an earring like Lindyral, but this wasn't a raven. He looked closer at it.

"It's a nightingale," she said.

"Who are you?"

"The Oracle of Arabeth," she said.

Something about her unnerved him. She felt familiar. "You're not the Oracle, you're a Fate. Why are you here?"

She nodded. "I'm your Fate. Lindyral should not have let that piece of information loose. As for why I am here, you came to me. I should be asking why you are here."

"I didn't come here for me. In fact, I was about to leave," he said.

"You don't have any questions for me?" she asked, raising an eyebrow.

"I do have questions, but they seem a bit pointless, now." He kicked at a stone embedded in the ground.

The woman frowned. "Are you so sure?"

"She made me promise to leave, to save myself. But I'm not sure anymore what my life will be without her."

The Fate lifted herself onto a fallen log to sit. "I see," she said. "And a promise will stop you?"

"She made it clear." *Last night, she made it clear she wants you back.* He ignored the voice in his head.

"Then there is nothing else you would ask of me?"

Mendleson thought about it. He'd had so many questions last night, and now, he had the opportunity to get them answered. *Why aren't I asking those questions?*

"Yes," she said. "Why aren't you asking them?"

"You can read my mind? You know what I want to ask?"

"Yes, but I can't answer any question you don't actually ask. I'm here to help you, Mendleson. You and Henrietta."

Mendleson understood the familiarity, then. It was a family resemblance, a matter of carriage. "You're Henrietta's grandmother."

"I may have been, but I have no ties to her anymore."

"You gave her the vision that had her meet me."

The woman's eyes went wide. "Please, do not speak of it."

"Why not? Why did you do it?"

"Please, I do not want Lindyral to hear of it."

Another voice broke in. "It is too late for that, Essorin."

A look of fear crossed the woman's face as Lindyral stepped out from behind a tree.

"Please, I didn't mean to…"

"But you did. You interfered with my charge. You sent her the vision to meet with this man, didn't you."

Essorin nodded slowly. "It didn't harm anything, and it gave Mendleson a choice."

"What?" Mendleson asked, but the two Fates ignored him.

"It didn't harm anything? It only threw off all my work, and you knew it would. Henrietta would have jumped at the chance to become a Fate, had you not interfered. Instead, I had to expend far more of my energy than I should have to convince her."

"That's not what she wanted," Essorin said, seeming to recover herself. Her voice grew stronger as she spoke. "You never gave her a choice from the time she was born. She wanted love, and you took it away at every opportunity."

"Love was *not* her destiny, and you know it. You knew it when I gave you the choice. You repay me like this?"

Essorin hopped off the tree and stood toe to toe with

the taller Lindyral. "I was told when I was made that my task was to guide our charges, to give them opportunities to change their fate. You have *never* done that for Henrietta. You took every opportunity away from her. You made certain that she would only choose the way you wanted her to choose. What would Clothoro say if she knew?"

"You *dare!*"

Mendleson tried to get their attention. "Excuse me."

"I have been tasked with overseeing the sighted for a thousand years," Lindyral continued, completely ignoring Mendleson. She seemed to have forgotten he was even there.

"Maybe it's time for a change," Essorin said.

Mendleson was scared. He remembered the rush of the fire when Lindyral had grown angry at him. He didn't want to be around when the two of them started using more than words to fight.

"Excuse me," he said, raising his voice.

Lindyral turned on him. "You are not welcome here. Your part in this is over."

Essorin pushed her out of the way, and Lindyral, surprised, tripped backward over a stump. "If you wish to save her," Essorin said, "you must get to the Standing Stone before sunset, and you must get her to admit her love to you before the stone. If you can do that, when the wraiths come, do what they ask."

"What will they ask?"

~ 261 ~

"I cannot tell you that," she said. "I can only tell you that you must be strong and unwavering in your love for her, or you both will die."

Lindyral was getting to her feet behind Essorin. She had a dark look on her face.

"One last thing," he said. "Would I have died in the storm if I had not met Henrietta?"

"It was a possibility."

"Watch out!" Mendleson said, as he saw Lindyral reach up behind Essorin, to grab Essorin by the hair. But it was too late. Lindyral put an arm around Essorin's neck, and there was nothing the shorter woman could do.

"If this is what you wish," Lindyral said, "If you wish to die for her, then go. Die for her."

The two Fates vanished, leaving Mendleson standing alone in the forest.

He didn't hesitate. He did have a chance to save her after all, and he knew what he had to do. He hoped he could get there in time and could somehow convince Henrietta to admit that she loved him.

His heart pounded just thinking about it. He hadn't imagined a few weeks ago that his life could change so much. He hadn't imagined that he could fall in love again, but he had. He had, and she was in danger.

A thread of fear ran through him that she would be too stubborn to admit it, too stubborn to risk his life to save hers.

"No," he said. "Don't think that way. If you get there, you'll find a way to save her.

He ran out of the woods, splashed across the stream, and entered the Oracle's hut. It was empty. Henrietta had already left.

He ran out the door, found the trail, and followed it, hoping he could catch her before twilight.

‡

At first, nothing happened. She'd expected the wraiths to show up and take her the moment the sun touched the horizon, but the plateau remained empty.

She walked over to it, put her hand on it. The stone was still warm from the sun. She felt a small tingle in her fingertips as she ran them across the runes that were carved into the surface.

She heard a noise among the trees again. A tremor of fear ran through her. *This is it,* she thought, and she turned to face the wraiths she knew were coming.

I'll stand my ground. I won't show fear.

The plateau was empty.

"Hello!" she called. "Hello?"

A few slow seconds passed. She could hear her breath in her ears. The sun had sunk lower, and the light was beginning to fade.

With a crash of branches, someone broke free from the treeline near the path and ran out onto the plateau.

Her breath caught in her throat. She could only see the outline of the man, as he stood against the backdrop of the sun, but it couldn't be anyone else.

"Mendleson?"

He ran toward her, and she took a few steps forward. When he'd crossed about half the distance between them, she heard his voice call to her. "Henrietta! I made it. I know how to save you!"

Just then, dark shapes appeared at the edges of the plateau, just as they had in her vision. Mendleson stood, outlined by the setting sun, in just the spot where she knew they would overwhelm him.

"Mendleson!" she screamed. "Run!"

‡

The path to the Standing Stone proved more arduous than Mendleson had anticipated. He'd been able to run at first, but it went uphill very quickly. Between rocks, fallen trees, and the general steep rise of the path, he didn't think he was catching up to Henrietta at all.

When the sun had sunk low in the sky, he began to despair of getting there in time. He feared that he would arrive on the plateau and find her corpse at the foot of the Stone.

And then he worked his way around a bend in the path to find a last climb ahead of him. He hoped he wasn't too late.

As quickly as he could, he climbed the last rocky slope. When he got to the top, he stood among the trees that ringed the edge while he caught his breath and looked for Henrietta.

He found her, standing near a massive monument of a stone that nearly tripled Henrietta's height. Its black faces were covered in runes of a sort, and in the glow of the setting sun, it appeared to shimmer with a strange sort of energy. He had a feeling that it was waiting for something, or someone.

And then Henrietta called out. "Hello! Hello?"

He waited for a moment, looking around, looking at her, taking the vision of her in. He had loved his wife, and he dearly and truly missed her, but the weeks he and Henrietta had been on the road had forged something even stronger in him, and he hoped between them. Watching her, as her half expectant, half fearful face glowed in the last light of the sun, only brought home to him that his original goal, to help this woman because he had failed Mirrielle, had become a desire to help this woman because he couldn't imagine doing anything else.

He ran out onto the plateau.

"Mendleson?" she asked, an almost unbelieving tenor in her voice.

She probably doesn't believe it. She thought I left.

"Henrietta!" he yelled across the distance between them. "I made it. I know how to save you!"

Henrietta stiffened, and a look of fear came over her. She wasn't looking at him, she was looking past him.

He turned around and saw for the first time the view beyond the lip of the plateau. It would have taken up all of his attention, but for the movement at the edges of the treeline, and the dark shapes that emerged.

Wraiths. I'm too late!

"No. No, I'm not."

He turned and ran for Henrietta. He only had to reach her before the wraiths, he only had to get her to declare her love for him, he only had to trust that she did love him.

As he took the first steps toward her, she took a step back. "Mendleson!" she screamed. "Run!"

He looked around and realized that the wraiths weren't coming for her, they were coming for him.

He put all his effort into running to Henrietta, but the wraiths were too quick. They swarmed over him, their hissing voices telling him to stop, telling him to give in. "Mendleson," they said, almost as one, "will you give what you must for her?"

He struggled against them, but they were too strong. He was without his sword, having forgotten it in his rush to catch Henrietta. They weren't attacking him like the others had before. They were holding him, their cold hands on his arms binding like shackles.

"Will you give what you must?"

Through the swarm of wraiths, he caught one last

sight of Henrietta, and she had tears in her eyes. *She saw this,* he thought. *This was her vision, her fate, our fate.*

How can I change it? How can I get her to declare her love?

And then he remembered what Essorin had said. *Do what the wraiths ask.*

He relaxed in their grip. This was why he had come. "Yes," he said. "I will give anything for her."

"It is done," said the chorus of hisses.

A hand came up to his face, the palm, covering his eyes.

At first, there was no difference. But all too sudden, pain lanced through his eyes and into his head. *This is when I die,* he thought.

"Henrietta!" he shouted, hoping she could hear him, hoping he was really speaking and not just imagining it. "Henrietta, I love you!"

He saw a burst of light, for a moment, and then everything went black and time stopped.

‡

Henrietta stood and watched as the wraiths closed in on him, just as she had seen. He had tried to run to her, but the wraiths quickly surrounded him, and he had stopped.

In her vision, she had always seen herself, standing, watching, until they left him and came for her. She had let it happen.

Only, the first time, it was different. She hadn't felt anything for him. Now, watching it for real, watching it happen in front of her, she felt her heart breaking, knowing that there was nothing she could do.

And she didn't understand why it hurt so much. Others in her life had died, her mother, her aunt, her uncle, her grandmother. Each one had hurt, but they had mostly hurt because she blamed herself for their deaths. Her grandmother had tried to tell her different, but Henrietta had known better.

This time, she couldn't blame herself. She'd done everything she could to drive him away, to make him leave her, even at the end when she didn't want him to go. Even when she needed him.

Yet, here he was, by his own choice. She shouldn't feel any responsibility. It shouldn't hurt this much that she knew he was going to die.

She took a step forward without understanding why.

Another step.

Her heart beat so that she could feel its pressure in her neck, behind her eyes.

Another step.

You must change your heart. A voice in her head. A voice who had never said those words to her. It sounded like her grandmother.

One more step.

What am I doing? I can't stop these things. But, somehow, it didn't matter. She decided that she couldn't allow him to sacrifice for her. And this time, the why of it had changed. This time, she knew she only wanted him to live, not for herself, but for him. Not because she would blame herself, but because he deserved to live. Because he had already helped her.

"Henrietta!" His voice called out to her from amidst the blackness of the wraiths.

And it was then that she realized why it hurt so much. It was then that she broke into a run, that she defied her vision of herself standing, waiting.

"Henrietta, I love you!"

She ran as if her life depended on it, but she already knew she would die. She ran to hold him one last time, to feel his touch.

She struck the back of a wraith as hard as she could, hoping she could break through to Mendleson. "I love you, Mendleson!" she cried as she collided with it. "I'm coming!"

She caught a glimpse of him laying on the ground, his eyes closed, as the wraiths turned to ward off her attack. She felt defeated, but she fought even more.

She punched one in the face, and felt the bones in her hand crack as she made contact. She didn't care. The pain in her hand could not compete with the pain in her heart.

She hit another, breaking yet more bones.

She felt herself grabbed from behind, her arms pulled back. She tried to kick out at the dark monster in front of her, but missed.

"Mendleson!"

She could see him better now, but she couldn't tell if he was breathing.

"Mendleson! Please!"

And then the sobs came. Great wracking pains followed by tears. She could hardly catch her breath. The cold arms that bound her, and held her in place, held her up. If they hadn't, she would have fallen to the ground.

"You killed him!" she managed to say between sobs.

They ignored her, and spun her around so that she could no longer see him.

Instead, through her tears, she saw the Standing Stone, lit from within, the glyphs shining as if they were on fire.

The wraiths brought her to it. She didn't fight them. She couldn't fight them. Even at the end, when she had changed, when she had seen what she'd done, even then, she hadn't changed her fate. *I love you Mendleson.*

And there, she decided what her answer to the Stone would be.

The wraiths stopped their movement toward the stone when she was close enough to reach out and touch it. Standing so close, the light from the glyphs was blinding. She had to shut her eyes.

"Touch it," she heard from a hissing voice. One of the wraiths behind her had spoken. "Touch it."

Henrietta didn't understand why it was different in this place, why they didn't just put a hand to her forehead like before and take her sight. And she didn't understand why she had to touch the stone.

But she did as they asked. The stone was cold and smooth under her fingers, like glass.

There you are, said a voice in her head. *I have been waiting for you.*

"Waiting for me?" she said between sobs.

Come, don't cry. You have choices. For the second time, she thought it was her grandmother speaking in her head.

"I don't want choices," she said. "I want Mendleson to live."

For yourself?

"Oh." *I want to spend eternity with him,* was her first thought, though she knew it was impossible.

Are you sure you wouldn't rather be a Fate? You could live forever.

"I do not want to live forever without Mendleson."

Done. I am proud of you.

The wraiths pulled her away from the stone.

"Wait," she cried out. "What does that mean?"

She didn't get an answer.

A wraith stepped between her and the stone. It put a hand up to her forehead, and it began to draw something out of her, just like the other times. As she slipped away into blackness, she thought she heard her grandmother's voice one last time. *The gift must still pass.*

But her last thought was of Mendleson. *I'm coming, my love.*

TWENTY-THREE

Henrietta opened her eyes. She hadn't expected she'd feel them open when she was dead. She hadn't expected, really, to open her eyes at all. The Fates were often clear as to what happened in life, but not a Seer that had ever been known was able to see beyond it.

Which explained why...

Which explained what? She couldn't remember what she had just been about to think. She tried for moments to remember, but wherever that thought was going to lead, she had lost the strand.

She sat up. Around her, she saw a familiar space. A small hut where she'd met the Oracle.

"I'm not dead," she said.

Was it a dream? Another vision? She didn't think so. It had seemed too real. The pain, too great.

And then she remembered. Mendleson, dead at the hands of the wraiths, and she started to cry. She realized, in that moment, that he had accomplished his goal, that he had set out to save her, and had succeeded. *But at what cost, Mendleson? What cost to you? What cost to me?*

She missed him already.

A hand touched her on her arm, and she jumped off the pallet she had been sleeping on. Her heart raced.

She hadn't even noticed the man sleeping next to her. She hadn't noticed Mendleson sleeping next to her.

Instead of slowing down, her heart raced even faster.

She rushed back onto the cot and hugged him. He was warm. "You're alive!"

She kissed his forehead as he began to sit up. The blanket slid down his bare chest. She pulled him against her and felt his skin upon hers. Her tears of sorrow became tears of joy.

She pulled back a bit to look at his face.

He opened his eyes for the first time, and she gasped.

His eyes were white. "You're blind," she said.

She ran her hand through his hair, and realized she didn't care.

"It's all right," he said. "It was the price I paid for you. I would have given a lot more."

"But..."

He put his fingers to her lips, quieting her. He found them easily, which surprised her.

"Henrietta," he said, "don't be sad. They didn't take everything. I am blind when you are not near me, but when you are close, I can see all that I need to see."

Henrietta was confused. "What do you mean?"

He lay back down and pulled her down with him. He put his hand on her bare back and massaged it. His other hand pulled her head to him and he kissed her, warm, strong, and deep. A spark seemed to exist between them, a connection that she didn't understand, but it ran down the length of her body as his legs pulled hers to him.

"When you are close," he said, pulling away only far enough to let the words come out, "I can see you."

About The Author

Mark Fassett lives in western Washington with his wife, children, and cats. He's had extensive experience in the mobile game business and was involved with some of the top selling titles at the time of their release, including multiple Duke Nukem Mobile games and Guitar Hero World Tour Mobile. He's also played and written music most of his life, and was "this close" to actually making money at it.

Find Me Online

Blog - http://www.markfassett.com
Twitter - http://twitter.com/mark_fassett

The Sacrifice of Mendleson Moony was written using StoryBox. StoryBox is software I developed specifically for writing fiction. You can try it for free at http://www.storyboxsoftware.com